Frederick William Robinson

**Slaves of the Ring**

Or, before and after. Vol. 2

Frederick William Robinson

**Slaves of the Ring**
*Or, before and after. Vol. 2*

ISBN/EAN: 9783337411305

Printed in Europe, USA, Canada, Australia, Japan

Cover: Foto ©Andreas Hilbeck / pixelio.de

More available books at **www.hansebooks.com**

OR,

# BEFORE AND AFTER.

BY

THE AUTHOR OF

" GRANDMOTHER'S MONEY," " WILDFLOWER,"
" UNDER THE SPELL,"

ETC., ETC.

" Le plus libre du monde est esclave à son tour."—THEOPHILE.

" Let none too hastily conclude that all goodness is lost, though it may for
a time be clouded and overwhelmed."—RAMBLER.

IN THREE VOLUMES.
VOL. II.

LONDON:
HURST AND BLACKETT, PUBLISHERS,
SUCCESSORS TO HENRY COLBURN,
13, GREAT MARLBOROUGH STREET.
1862.
The right of Translation is reserved.

# BOOK II.

## "Love Matters."

[CONTINUED.]

"Under the rose, there was a gentleman
Came in at the wicket."
                                        CHAPMAN.

"Is this your sweetheart? I had need wish you much joy, for I see but a
little towards."
                                        HEYWOOD.

# SLAVES OF THE RING;

OR,

## BEFORE AND AFTER.

---

## CHAPTER X.

GREY'S CASE.

I HAD much to perplex me on my way back
to the Farm. The hasty departure of Thirsk,
the hurried confession he had made me, and
the reservation that had lurked in the midst
of his apparent confidence. That he kept
something back, that it was his nature to
hide something in the secret recesses of a
heart that would never beat calmly and
equably, I was convinced.

And yet I was convinced, too, that it all
might have been so different; that his was a
nature which had run wild, and had had no
generous culture; and so, to quote his own

mocking words, had put forth evil fruit. There must have been a time, there *was* a time when a word in the right season would have turned him from the path he was pursuing, and led him on to better things; but the real friends were few, and indolent or im-perceptive—and so from bad to worse, and all the fair young shoots trodden in the dust. For there were flashes, at times, of a fair thought, an honest impulse yet; and though he drove on with the adverse wind and sea, some faint effort to resist still shone forth, if at uncertain intervals. I suppose there never was a noble nature utterly cast down and rendered vile. From the abyss must wail forth, at times, some regret for the misspent past that has ended in such ruin.

Why I should have these gloomy thoughts on my return, was a matter of some doubt; he had left me in good spirits, sanguine as to the result of his enterprise, and rejoiced to be quit of farming life and adventure.

True, he had spoken little of passion, and a great deal of the money that his scheming would bring him; and my own love troubles had set in, and, perhaps, tinged me with a hue not wholly unromantic.

There is a romantic episode in most men's lives, and I, at least, did not escape. When my hand was on the farm-house gate, I thought of the warning with which Thirsk had favoured me, and wondered how he had guessed a secret only self-confessed but a short while since. As if to eyes commonly observant such secrets can be kept, when a whisper, look, or blush will throw one "moon-struck" off his guard!

It was late for the folk at Welsdon, and only Mr. Genny was sitting up for me—a substitute for his niece which I did not particularly admire.

" Ye be late, lad."

" I saw him off by the nine p.m. train."

" To Loondon ?"

" Yes."

"So there's an end of a harebrained young mon, who will ne'er do any good in the world," commented Genny; "I reckon I needn't sit up with my gun to-noight, Mr. Neider."

"You suspect him still?"

"Ay—and I have suspected him some toime for the matter of that, though I went a blundering way to foind him out. There be your supper, lad."

"I don't care about supper to-night, thank you."

"Darm it, I shall save by ye supperless people!" cried he; "this Thirsk maun have turned all your stomachs. There's Grey gone upstairs as white as a ghost."

"Indeed!"

"And Harriet's oot of temper, and ye won't have any supper. We're getting moighty cheerful here. Why, *I* bean't even quite myself."

"I'm sorry to hear it."

'There ha' been such a stir up to-day aboot

one thing and the oother—dogs, and nieces, and Thirsk. And how that girl Ricksworth troobles me, too !"

"Indeed !"

"Don't go up just this moment, now. Ye're a sensible koind of lad, take you altogether. Not quite so much nonsense aboot ye as most people of your age."

"Thank you for the compliment," I said, laughing.

"Do *ye* think, now—sit doon, lad, sit doon—that I was hard on the girl? She worries me."

And he leaned his elbow on his knee, and clasped his odd-shaped forehead with his hand.

"There might have been a better, a milder way of telling Mercy her services were not required, perhaps."

"I'm not a foine gentleman, with foine words always ready," said he; "my education bean't much to brag of, and I speak fair and short, and to the purpose.

But Harriet says I was hard on her; that she is as much my niece as herself—which be true enough—and—and in fact that I was more than rough to her. She forgets how I have been put out all day."

"Mercy may come round in the morning."

"Not she—she has an awful spirit of her own, and always has had. It'll bring her to trooble some day. Now, look here, Mr. Neider."

He began to beat time with one hand on the other.

"I'm a man of my woord, and I worn't ha' her without a character. I doan't doobt her, moind ye, but we Gennys be a little obstinate—all but one poor deevil of our stock, who'll be here in the race week—and if she says noa, I say noa, and stick to it. Still, if she goes to London, as she talks aboot, I should loike to help her with a poond or two. It's hard to have one's hand always in one's pocket, but if I thought nobody would know it, I shouldn't mind a couple—of—poonds."

He drawled the words out as though they were a couple of pounds of flesh, he thought of disposing to some-one in the Shylock line of business.

" Harriet maun't know it," he said, suddenly.

" Oh !"

" We've had a bit of a quarrel to-night —an up-and-downer, for a change. Lord! we haven't wrangled now a year or more, but she be awful hot when she thinks anybody's in the wrong, and I've been sharper than I meant, too. And so, if ye could manage to meet — accidently loike — my niece, Mercy, to-morrow or next day, ye moight tell her there's no offence taken or meant—and there's her passage to London, or something till she gets a place. Two poonds, didn't I say ?"

And he began rummaging in his trousers pocket. My first impulse was to reject the commission which he was anxious to thrust upon me; I was almost a stranger to the Ricksworths—the office was not a grateful one, and I had some doubts whether his niece would accept the proffered gift. His next remark, however, altered my determination.

"Ye may see the moother if ye loike, and let her keep it for Mercy till she goes away, or spend it if she stays too long at home. If Ricksworth be in the way, leave the matter to a better toime. Ye doan't moind, now?"

"No, sir."

"Ay!—ye're a good lad."

And he dropped two sovereigns into my hand.

"And I'm thinking we've wasted a good deal of candle-loight—good noight, Mr. Neider."

"Good night, sir."

I went to my room, where I was surprised to find William Grey sitting on the corner of his bed, with a very tumbled head of hair, and a face colourless and blank.

"Why, Grey, what's the matter?"

"Shut the door, there's a good fellow," he said, quickly, "or old Genny will hear you."

"Is anything wrong?" I asked, after closing the door, as directed.

"I have made a fool of myself—that's all."

"That's an affliction that will befall each of us in turn."

"What consolation is that to me?"

"Not much—just at present."

"Neider, I never could keep a secret— I'm going to let you into this one."

More confidence!—more love affairs!— would this night of incident never be at an end? I should be glad to sleep upon it all, and wake up in the morning less burdened with other people's trouble.

"It's soon told, so don't look so weary over it," said he; "it's all been brought about by that old brute!"

"Ricksworth?"

"No—Genny—*her* uncle."

"Oh!—go on."

"I couldn't stand it any longer, so I went out after them, and followed them to their cottage, at the back of the village—we've passed it fifty times, you know—and asked to see Mercy, and,"—with a great gulp down of something in his throat—"saw her."

"Grey, you were never so hasty?"

"I always strike whilst the iron's hot, and my heart was full—and, God knows, I had loved her long enough."

"It's an ill-starred love, Grey—the more I think of it, the more I feel certain. And she accepted you?"

"Accepted me!" cried Grey, "as if I should be sitting here a miserable devil, all gooseflesh, if she had."

"Refused you?—refused you?" I repeated twice.

I could not understand it; here was a chance in life for Mercy Ricksworth; such as she could have hardly expected—a young,

good-looking, well-to-do man, whose unselfish heart had chosen her before the
world.

"I asked her very plainly, very earnestly,
to be my wife—I told her I might be my
own master almost at any time, and that my
family would be glad to think her one of
them. And she dashed down every hope
by an angry 'No,' that came like a thunderbolt upon me. So it's all over."

"It is best, Grey,"

"Well, it's easy to say that, if not to
think so."

"Years hence, you will thank your stars
for the escape."

"I told you once I never changed—I
shan't in this case, where I have felt the most
deeply. Oh! Neider I have seen so much
to love in that girl; beneath the surface of
a hasty, excitable temperament, there is such
deep, true feeling—such earnest thought for
others. For all but me, from whom she
turns away!"

" Courage, you are young, and will not break your heart over this."

"I shall never forget her, Neider—my love was a slow growth, and its roots struck deep. And you *will* think it a hasty dash on my part, because you know so little of me," he added petulantly.

" May I ask a question ? "

" Fifty—I am ashamed of nothing."

" Did she ever encourage you?—lead you on to think that she might return your affection ? "

" How could she know I loved her, before I confessed all to-night, and frightened her out of her wits ! " he cried.

" She might have guessed it, in all probability."

" Well, I thought she knew at times, and then I didn't think so—sometimes she was low-spirited, then she was light-hearted and almost a sister to me—and then she was like a spoiled child, and then all sunshine again.   Oh ! "

And he doubled his fist and punched his pillow savagely.

"I'm off to London next week, Neider— or the week after, perhaps," he added, with a reluctant sigh.

"I shall be sorry to part with you."

"The place will give me the horrors now, and I shall never learn to grin at what every fool tells me is fancy, till I've settled down in my lonely bachelor's farm.  I wish I could hear of a little place, Cumberland way—there would be a chance of dodging the creeps near you."

"Cumberland is a dull place, Grey."

"Can't you sell the farm, and go partners with me in a bigger one in a more cheerful part of England, then?  With your mother for housekeeper, we two old bachelors could get on very well together."

"We two old bachelors!—how soon you settle matters, Grey."

"I tell you I shall never marry—and I don't believe you will."

" Why not ? "

" You're too matter-of-fact.  A German
doll, solid and wooden, that will wear well,
and take little impression."

" Better so than——"

" That's right, old fellow ! " cried Grey,
seeing that I paused; "spare me, now I am
down on my back, and clean floored for
the nonce."

" You'll go quietly to bed now, Grey ? "

" Well, it will not mend matters sitting
up ? "

And Grey went to bed, and slept rest-
lessly that night, and once cried out in his
sleep, " I shan't forget her !"—and so kept
me restless too.

His was a strange contrast to the passion
of Nicholas Thirsk—I thought that night
that there was little doubt where the truest
love and the most unselfish thoughts were.

# CHAPTER XI.

## MY MISSION.

THE cottage of Peter Ricksworth, black sheep, nestled in a hollow at the back of the village—a rickety wooden edifice, standing alone in its glory, and therefore convenient to society in general, which escaped the many oaths that rolled forth from open door and window at all hours of the day and night. A cottage where Peter Ricksworth spent most of those hours not devoted to the taproom of the Haycock Inn—very much in the way within doors, and far from an ornament without, with a bent hat

cocked on one side of his head, and a
grimy black pipe in his mouth.

Peter Ricksworth scarcely did a stroke of
honest work from year's end to year's end;
a man with a worse character could not
have been found in any village within fifty
miles of Welsdon in the Woods. A man
more often drunk from money he had
stolen from his wife's hard earnings, more
often disputatious and villainously quarrel-
some, more often locked up for breaking
the peace and other people's heads, it would
have been impossible to find.

There was not a tradesman in the village,
a farmer or landowner beyond it, that
would not have shrunk from engaging
Peter Ricksworth; only in the harvest
time, when hands were scarce, and every
day the corn lay in the fields there
were many hundred pounds at stake, he
found a job occasionally, and cut slices
out of some one with his reaping-hook.
But of late he had done nothing, and still

lived, and save looking a trifle more lank and gaunt, was the same Peter Ricksworth who had been a nuisance to the village from the time he took to drinking, fifteen years ago. Rumour said that his wife had driven him to it by her unsociability and eternal preaching, worrying, and discomfort—but Peter Ricksworth had not required driving, and had gone his " wilful gait " with perfect ease. Rumour said also that he lived now by poaching on the Freemantle preserves, and snaring rabbits and hares in the warrens of the landed gentry; and rumour was true in this respect, and did him no injustice.

Still this busy rumour, that has so much to say of all of us, and says so little that is true and just, gave him credit for no virtue, and cast no light upon the rugged character living at Welsdon's end. Nothing was known of the intense affection for the only one who tried to cast some ray of comfort in his way—of the father's love for the child of his miserable union. An affection that was, on the whole, undemonstrative, and but exhibited itself when a word was said against her; that was reciprocated by her, who saw how every man's back was turned against her father, and knew alone of all the world the tortuous way to that man's better nature.

I found the cottage only occupied by Mrs. Ricksworth—a fortunate occurrence, as I deemed, for the disposal of Mr. Genny's two pounds—and Mrs. Ricksworth in pattens at the door, washing sundry garments in an immense tub, that necessitated a " header " of the good lady's every time the soap was in demand.

" Good morning, Mrs. Ricksworth."

" Good morning to you," with a critical glance from each side of her hooked nose; " you're from the farm ?"        .

I answered in the affirmative.

" I saw you last night with the others. Is there any news ?"

"Mr. Genny wished me to call. He is rather uneasy about his niece, Mercy."

"Ah! she's a fool, maybe, and blind to her own interest."

"She spoke of seeking a situation in London, and he thought if she would accept a couple of sovereigns——"

"She'd fling it in his face, more likes than not. She's getting more like her father every day, I fear. I'm sure I've worked hard, and loved my bible, and done my best—but it's all agin' me still."

The voice was not musical, or despondent—but there was a hidden pathos even in its harshness. She had done her best; but it was not given her to know when was the best time, the fairest opportunity, and so had seen her work spoil. There are many like her amongst the medley of human life in which we move.

"Mr. Genny, being doubtful if Mercy would accept the gift, has left it to me to place the amount at your disposal. You

might take care of it, and offer it as from
yourself—or it might help to lessen the
expenses incurred by her present stay with
you."

"He's very good—and he's a rich man,
who can afford the money.   Where is it?"

And her cold grey eyes looked towards
my hand that held the gift.   I placed it
within her horny palm, after she had wiped
it carefully with her checked apron.   She
looked very much like her brother, as she
turned the money slowly in her hands.

"I'll hide it in the old chancy tea-pot,
I'm thinking," she said; and then turning
to me, "and tell Matthew it shall all be
spent on the girl, whether she leaves home
or not—every farthing of it!"

"Is it likely she will go to London, do
you think?"

"I don't know—I'm not in her confidence—she tells me nothing.   If her mind
is set on going, she will go."

"I am sorry to hear she is so headstrong."

"I don't see that it matters to you," she returned, with a curious stare over her tub at me; "but perhaps it's a compliment, which don't suit me, for I've no taste for it. She's a good girl in her way, not a mother's girl—that luck worn't to be expected."

She went into the room, and proceeded to dispose of her unlooked-for acquisition in some secret receptacle, whilst I slowly retraced my way to the Farm.

Twenty yards from Ricksworth's cottage, I came upon Peter Ricksworth and his daughter—a fair picture of "Beauty and the Beast"—arm-in-arm together.

Mr. Ricksworth's eyes widened a little at my appearance in the green lanes, so close to his house; his daughter affected not to see me.

"Good for the een to see one of Mr. Genny's fine gentlemen so nigh us," said he, at the top of his voice, as usual; "you've brought a message from the farmer?"

Seeing that I hesitated, he said,

" And something more than a message, mayhap; for there be times after harvest when an odd pound can be screwed out of old Genny."

" I came with an inquiry from Mr. Genny."

" What was that? " and Mercy looked up for the first time.

" He wished to ask if you really intended to go to London."

" We're all going to London to make our fortun's," said Ricksworth; "open a beer shop, p'raps, with me to do the cellar work, and Mercy the barmaid business, and the old woman to see nobody don't pay twice."

" Father, we can do something better than jest at our ill luck," and Mercy passed on with her parent, who muttered,

" Right again, my girl, and so we can. Dashed if you ain't always right, my pretty face ! "

I was some two or three hundred yards

further on my way when Mercy Ricksworth
overtook me.

"I have come back to ask you a question
—one or two," she said, speaking very
rapidly; "my uncle sent you here with
something more than an inquiry?"

"He is not unwilling to take you into
his service, Mercy, if——"

"That will do," she interrupted; "I don't
wish to hear the conditions—I never desired
to become his servant. There is one niece
too many already at Follingay Farm,"
she added, with some little natural
jealousy.

I say natural jealousy, for Harriet Genny
was not more closely allied to the farmer than
the girl at my side, and one was her uncle's
confidant and housekeeper — perhaps his
heiress—and the other had been refused a
dairymaid's place. It seemed unfair, at first
sight, though no man in the world is
expected to support *all* his nephews and
nieces.

"Do you bring a message from anyone else?" she asked.

She looked so steadily at me that I coloured.

"I have not seen Miss Genny this——"

"Don't prevaricate—you know I don't allude to my cousin, and I'm not ashamed to say whom I mean. Have you brought a message from William Grey, sir?"

"Had I done so, I should have delivered it," was my reply.

"William Grey is one who could not keep a secret for his life sake. He has told you all; I can read it all upon your face."

"You are a shrewd physiognomist."

"And he is a babbler—a poor weak babbler, that is not deserving a thought."

Her contemptuous manner irritated me.

"I am afraid you do not understand him."

"He is easy to read, too."

"His true heart and his deep feelings are not easily understood or appreciated, nevertheless."

" You are his friend ? "

"I am proud to say I am."

" And he has told you of—of a very silly wish of his? "

" I see no reason to deny it. He has."

" And is it possible—do you really think that he is grieving for me—the daughter of Peter Ricksworth ? "

" It is more than possible."

"Tell him not to grieve," she cried impetuously, " he will be a fool all his life to give a second thought concerning me. Tell him I never loved him, thought of him—tell him I hated him, if it will drive me out of his thoughts. You men have some way of consoling each other for imaginary trials !"

" He will recover, Mercy, in good time."

" To be sure," she continued, in the same wild tone ; " I should be sorry to think he would not recover. If he should speak of me again, tell him that my girlish folly and vanity—I was only sixteen—has been the cause of this, and that I am very, very sorry for it. Tell him, too, that I was sorry directly I saw how far it had led him, and did my best to check him, and show him what a poor girl I was, and how unworthy of him. I was his best friend after all!"

I regarded her with some surprise.

"I knew what was best for him. If I had loved him, I could have only brought him disgrace and shame, and he would have soon tired of me; and—and—as I did *not* love him—please, tell him that, sir—I did not sink my chance of happiness with his own, for the sake of being a farmer's wife."

"Your refusal is creditable to you, Mercy," said I; "many girls in your position would have tried very hard to secure William Grey for a husband."

"Do you taunt me with my position, too?" and she drew herself up haughtily.

" I hope you think more worthily of me than that. I did not imply a taunt—I am sorry that you fancy my words conveyed one."

" I am inclined to judge hastily—forgive me, sir. I am a young woman alone in the world, striving hard to do my duty—I am desolate, and in trouble!"

" Mercy Ricksworth!"

I turned suddenly upon her, but she was hurrying back towards her home. I made one step towards her, but she waved me back with a quick hand, and a look on her face that offered a faint resemblance to her father's.

It was a look that checked my progress, and dismissed a doubt which had crept to my mind whilst she was speaking. Wayward and ungovernable as she appeared, I thought that William Grey had had a lucky escape, and that the first disappointment was, after all, the best. Every step that took me further from Welsdon's End strengthened me in that conviction.

# CHAPTER XII.

## MY TURN.

HARRIET GENNY was awaiting my arrival at
the farm-house. Her uncle and Mr. Grey
had gone over the land, and she was there
alone to confront me. She was looking pale
and ill that morning.

"My uncle tells me you have been to my
aunt's—to the Ricksworths'," she said, seeing
that the relationship puzzled me for the
moment.

"Yes."

"With two sovereigns for Mercy," she
said, a little scornfully.

"Yes."

" And she took them ?"

" For the present she knows nothing about them—I have left them with her mother."

" You are becoming quite a go-between, Mr. Neider," was her next remark, which brought the blood to my cheeks.

" I was asked to accept the mission as a favour—and I accepted it, Miss Genny."

" And forestalled me ?"

" I beg your pardon — I was not aware——"

" You are aware of nothing, but that which is brought in capital letters before your eyes," she interrupted, crossly; " did it not strike you, at least, that I might take some common interest, as a cousin, in Mercy Ricksworth ?"

" I can but say I did not think of it."

" Did you think that I could not under-stand one whose nature is so similar to mine —whom I would love as a dear young sister, if she turned not so disdainfully away from me? Have I so much to endear me to this house, that my heart cannot yearn to that girl, and sympathize with her, and understand her? If I never had a sister of my own, it is the more reason that I would go far to make her like one!"

She was rebelling against the loneliness of her life, the unnaturalness of her position there, the want of sympathy and love to be found within the farm-house walls. I could see it then, and I knew last night's quarrel with her uncle had helped to disturb the too even tenor of her way.

"Tell me the result of your mission," she demanded; and I was too much her servant in my heart to disguise it, had there even been a reason for so doing. I kept back my interview with Mercy—it was another story in which Grey played the principal part, and I had no right to allude, in any way, to *that*.

The story ended, she walked away from

me without another word, and left me to proceed to my day's work.

In the evening she made her appearance in the parlour, equipped for a journey.

"I am going to the Ricksworths'," she said to her uncle, who was studying his banker's cheque-book.

"Ay, lass, as ye will," said he, strangely humble.

After the storm was over, Genny was invariably sorry for his differences with his favourite niece—and that particular evening he would not have objected to anything.

"It's late, Miss Genny," I ventured to say; "surely you will not think of proceeding that distance alone, at so late an hour?"

"I am not afraid of the dark, sir—and I am too well known to be hurt."

"If you would allow me to accompany you as far as the cottage," I suggested.

"Ay—it's as well," added Genny, "there are queer characters aboot, now the race toime draws near—if ye don't moind Mr. Grey or Neider, Harriet ?"

Harriet turned quickly to Mr. Grey, who sat poring over a book, with a weary expression of countenance.

" I won't deprive Mr. Neider of the pleasure," said Grey, and Harriet frowned at him for his politeness.

There was nothing left but to accept my escort, unless Miss Genny wished to create a disturbance concerning a common act of courtesy; and shortly afterwards we were in the dark road, along which I had walked with Nicholas Thirsk last night.

Harriet Genny was a good walker, and went along at a rapid pace, declining the offer of my arm with a politeness so cold, that it had the reverse effect of making my blood boil. All the way there she declined to discuss any topic whatsoever, and few and far between were the monosyllables with which she responded to my artfully directed queries. And all my questions concerned

Mercy Ricksworth, in whom I knew now she took no common interest.

Before the cottage, which I had visited that morning.

"Will you wait here, Mr. Neider? I presume you have no wish to protect me from the danger that may beset me inside the house?"

"I will wait here, if you please."

And in no very amiable mood I waited for Harriet Genny, and wandered to and fro in the dark road, and listened to the rustle-rustle of the autumn leaves, and thought, take it all together, what a very cut-throat place it looked by starlight. It was a long conference; I heard the clock in Welsdon church tower chime the half-hour past eight, the three-quarters, strike nine, chime the quarter past. I began to have a dim suspicion, at last, that Harriet Genny had passed out by a side door through a lane at the back, and gone on her way alone in defiance of my politeness—which suspicion became finally so strong, that I stepped over the palings and across the patch of garden ground, with the intention of peeping through the lattice window, whence the light shone—the only sign of life before me.

It was very undignified, but my temper was aroused—there was a dogged, obstinate, pig-headed mood, to which I was subject at times—and I had an extreme objection to Harriet Genny stealing a march upon me. So I stooped and peered over Mrs. Ricksworth's window-blind.

My suspicions were confirmed; there were only two inmates in that room, Mercy Ricksworth and her mother; and there were three doors to the room—four or five, perhaps, for the place looked all doors. Mercy Ricksworth sat on a chair by a feebly flickering fire, nursing her chin with one hand, and rocking herself slowly to and fro; Mrs. Ricksworth was ironing at a table, her mob-cap coming so near the candle every moment, that, had I been less excited, my fears would have been aroused lest she should set her head on fire. Whilst I made quite sure that Harriet Genny was not in some remote corner of the room, I heard Mercy say,

" I thought she was a proud and upstart woman, and fancied herself above me—I've been wrong there."

" You're always wrong, I'm inclined to fancy."

" Well, I owned I was wrong."

" And you were as rude as ever owning it—like your wicked father."

" Do leave him alone just a minute, mother."

" You take after him more every day."

" Ah! talk about *me!* "

" And he hasn't his equal in the town, and we haven't heard the worst of him yet, and—ya-a-a-h!" screamed Mrs. Ricksworth, catching sight of my white face pressed against the glass, and dropping her flat iron in dismay, "here's the devil come to fetch him before his time!"

Mercy started up, and I beat a hasty retreat over the palings, and along the road. I heard the latch click, and the door open, but I was out of visual range by that time, and speeding on to the Farm. I knew where the narrow lane at the back of Genny's cottage met the high road again, and I made all haste towards it, and ran almost head-first into the pit of Peter Ricksworth's stomach.

"Cuss it! young earthquake, do you want to bust a man?" he bawled; "who the devil are you, knocking against honest men in the dark, and scaring all their wits away?"

And he leaned against the hedge-row to recover his breath.

"I beg pardon—but I was in a great hurry, and I wished to overtake Miss Genny."

"She's a little way ahead—I suspected it was my fine madam, by her drawing her dress closer to her, as though I was coming along the high road full-blown with the small-pox. Or," he said, after a pause, " she might have thought me drunk, not knowing that I have promised Mercy to keep sober as a judge this side of the race week. Not t'other side, you know," and by the star-light I could see the ruffian winking at me; " Lord love her, I couldn't promise her so much as that!"

" Good night to you."

" I was about to ax you what's become of Mr. Thirsty."

" If you mean Mr. Thirsk, he's gone to London."

" After Robin Genny, and both at their old tricks again by this time — the dare-devils!"

" Good night to you—good night."

" Oh! good night to you," he growled; " I'd been a mightier sight more civil, if I had doubled up a gentleman with *my* bullet-head."

I was on my way again, anathematizing
the delay. I ran through the village at a
rattling pace, to the amazement of the few
tradesfolk putting up their shutters, and
to the exasperation of a small dog that ran
barking at my heels, till I turned round
and kicked him.

At the other extremity of the village,
and in the green lanes again, I came up
with Harriet Genny.

"Why, you must have missed me, Mr.
Neider," she said, in the most innocent and
aggravating manner.

"Missed you, Miss Genny—I——"

She had struggled hard with her powers
of composure; but my heated face, shortness
of breath, and indignant looks were too
much for her, and she burst into a musical
peal of laughter, that first rendered me more
indignant and then made me laugh too.
It was so seldom that she laughed, and it
stood in this instance evidence of so keen
an enjoyment, that I could but soften and

laugh with her. And so we were very good
friends again.

"You see I have reached here without
molestation from the tramps on their way
to the races," she said; "it was a matter of
dispute between us whether country roads
were safe, I think?"

Her petulance had vanished, and she was
in her happiest mood—the moods lying so
few and far between, that I would not have
disturbed them by a word. Surely she was
born to be a happier, brighter woman, had
the force of circumstances set not too
strongly against her?

"I'm as variable as a March month, Mr.
Neider; I came out like a lion, and am going
home like a lamb."

"A frank confession."

"I feel really in high spirits to-night,
however," she explained; "I could sing,
along the highroad."

"Is it fair to ask the reason for the
change?"

"Oh! you noticed the stormy character of the early portion of this evening?"

"Ahem—I fancied it was a little cloudy."

"Candidly, am I not the worst-tempered woman you have ever met?"

"Candidly—no."

"Tell me of the ogress who surpassed me?"

"You have not answered my question yet."

"The reason for the change in me. Why, the great discovery that I had been misunderstood, and that amidst all Mercy's foolish jealousy there was a great deal of love for me at the bottom of her heart," replied Harriet; "and it was very pleasant to make the discovery, though she owned it with her old ungraciousness. Why, it's not such a sombre-tinted world after all! Perhaps I shall not always be in russet brown, and with a sad and woe-begone countenance.

For I *was* very light-hearted once, until some began to misunderstand me, and others to torture me, and others to hold me in eternal suspense. And some day, God willing, it may all be bright again—I can believe it will to-night. Why, I shall be going to the races next!"

"I hope so."

"Why do you hope so?"

"Because it would be very hard to leave you alone in the farm-house."

"Oh! I'm used to that—and I don't like races."

"I was hopeful that you would—just for once—have accepted my escort, if only for the little amends you owe me for running away to-night."

"I have never cared for races, although my uncle has pressed me every year to accompany him. Besides——"

"What?"

"Oh! nothing;" and I could see her colour as plainly by the friendly stars as I had seen Peter Ricksworth wink a quarter of an hour before.

" You will not go, then ? "

" If my uncle accompanies us, perhaps I will."

" Say you will."

" How you bother, to be sure ! "

" Well, say you will. It's the first and last time I shall ever have the pleasure of sharing your holiday — a year's pupilage will have passed before the races come round again."

" I had forgotten."

" Am I to hear you say 'yes'? "

" Oh !—*yes*, then."

Talk about happiness that night, I could have danced a fandango under the starlit heavens, or flung somersaults, or sung comic songs. I was all happiness, and prepared for any extravagance. My heart was full ; I was choking in the throat—there was an electric fluid running in every vein of my body. And how sweetly the " yes " had sounded—despite her feigned indifference to the question—and how beautiful she looked !

"Mind the road here, Miss Genny," I said, with great solicitude; "they have been shooting stones down to-day—will you take my arm just here ? "

And she placed her hand upon my arm at once, and my heart began to thump again so strangely—and it was dream-land once more, and I a figure wandering in it, dreaming within the dream that made me happy.

It was but a short way to the Farm; the late moon was beginning to peer over the roof that was so close at hand. And at every step my heart beat so hard that I was afraid she would hear it.

"On the wane," I murmured, almost involuntarily.

"What, the moon ?"

"No, the happy days here—the year of my apprenticeship, wherein I have made one or two friends, I hope."

" What a number !"

" If they are true ones, it is sufficient. Miss Genny, I count you amongst my friends—am I precipitate ?"

She gave a startled look into my face, and then answered in a voice that trembled,

" I don't bear you a great deal of malice."

" I wonder if you will be sorry to see the back of me—if, after I am gone, you will ever——"

" I shall be gone first."

" Miss Genny !"

Her face was very pale now, and her voice had a strange ring in it.

" I shall be gone first, perhaps," said she; "talking of goings and comings has brought me back to a strange world—and I had forgotten it."

" Going away !—when ?"

" Don't ask me—I don't know."

" But, Miss Genny—dear Miss Genny."

" Let go my hand, sir !—how dare you so forget yourself ?—how dare——"

She had wrenched her hand from my nervous clutch, and had dashed towards the farm-gate, which she shook wildly, in a vain effort to open. I was at her side again.

"Miss Genny, I have said too much, or too little. Miss Harriet, dear Harriet, I must tell you all. If you will only——"

"Mr. Neider," turning towards me, and speaking very calmly and distinctly, "you have said too much, and startled my confidence and trust in you. God knows what I have said or done to lead you on; and God forgive me if by a word or look I have encouraged in you any thought of me. Will you forget all this?—oh! will you promise for ever to forget this?"

"Miss Genny—I will try!"

A moment afterwards we entered the farm-house parlour together.

# CHAPTER XIII.

## TRAMLINGFORD RACES.

TRAMLINGFORD race-course was situated
some seven miles and a half from Welsdon
in the Woods, and about a mile and a
quarter from the ancient town of Tramlingford. A time-honoured institution was
Tramlingford races, and well patronized by
the nobility, gentry, and public in general,
as the circulars say. Patronized to a certain extent, under difficulties, for it always
rained Tramlingford race week, and, save
the few canvas booths, and the two race
stands, there was little chance of shelter in the
neighbourhood. More than once attempts

had been made to dodge the weather, by shifting it to late in August instead of late in September, but the wet season shifted also, and the rain came down all the more violently for the attempt to take advantage of it.

It was a curious inconsistency of human nature, that all race-goers made sure of fine weather year after year, and even started with great faith in it, and were invariably caught, on the road to Tramlingford, by opposing elements.

And the Tramlingford race week in particular, that came round during my stay at the Follingay Farm—wherein I had begun to live and learn what life was—set in no more favourably than its predecessors, and we left Welsdon in the Woods under gloomy auspices.

Mr. Genny's dog-cart was turned out for the occasion, and William Grey and I sat behind, whilst the farmer and his niece took the front seat—the farmer driving.

Harriet Genny had kept her promise, and there she was by the side of her uncle, in her quiet grey-silk holiday dress. Since that night when her mood had been so varied, and ended so strangely and sadly for myself, she had never spoken of her promise. The night preceding the great gathering of the county, she had expressed a wish to accompany her uncle, and he, surprised at the suggestion, could but say " Ay," and assent.

We were very good friends now, Harriet Genny and I ; but it was a friendship distinct from anything that had gone before, that kept me at a distance, and burnt me up with fever. Towards me there were no longer those varied moods that I had thought so trying to the temper, and that I knew now had had a charm to lure the best feelings of my heart away. Before the night on which I had betrayed myself, she had been capricious, excitable, and abrupt; succeeding that period there had been one even current, which there was no disturbing or resisting. It carried me away, despite myself, and set me at a distance from her; after that there were no half confidences, no more little quarrels that required explanation and—forgiveness! She might have been a sister, who loved and pitied me for some infirmity under which I laboured, she was so gentle in her manners. It was as if she were striving to make amends for something which had deceived me; it was a pitying gentleness, that galled me and rendered me unhappy. Still, there was no fighting against it, and my efforts to bring her back to her old self were as futile as though I had attempted to bring back last year's spring.

And it was all my own fault—I knew that, I felt all that; I should have waited for a better time, and kept my lips sealed, and my heart closed. At the best, I was but a friend of a few months, and had no right to dash hastily forward with professions that could but naturally alarm her.

"God knows what I have said or done to lead you on," she had said, when first aroused to all that she had given birth to in my heart, and her voice faltered, and the tears were in her eyes. She could feel for my distress, but she could not love me in return, and, like William Grey, I must live my passion down.

So it was a party not the most hilarious that was proceeding to Tramlingford Heath in search of a day's amusement—three out of the four were at least of a thoughtful turn, and Mr. Genny was grim and stern, and cut somewhat spitefully at his horse's ears. Even Ipps, jogging on the old mare in advance, appeared to have caught the infection, or have fallen asleep on the way, he hung his head so low.

The heavy banks of clouds that had been rising from the west were now gathering over the whole sky, and one or two heavy rain-drops warned us of the first shower. Grey and I spread a second rug over our

knees, and buttoned our great-coats to the
chin—Genny struggled to fix his chaise
umbrella—Harriet drew her shawl closer
round her and shivered.

" It is a miserable day," she murmured ;
" if I were of a superstitious turn of mind,
I should fancy something was going to
happen."

" Ay—and I'm darmed if it woan't be
the horrors," said Genny ; " 'pon my
soul, I never went to the races with such a
a dead-and-alive lot in my life !"

" Oh ! it's the wet weather," cried Grey,
who took the hint to himself; " we shall
have these heavy winds, and these heavy
showers, all day—and it's up-hill work to be
jolly in the midst of them."

" I wonder if Sir Richard Freemantle
will be on the course," said Harriet, starting
a topic of her own.

" I hope so," said her uncle.

" Do you wish to see him, uncle ? "

" Ay."

Harriet looked at Mr. Genny, but he did not appear inclined to offer any explanation, and when she had given up the thought of it his answer came.

"I said the foirst time I saw Sir Richard I'd put a question to him, for my own credit's sake, if not for my niece, Mercy's— and I'll keep my word, moind ye. I always do."

"But Sir Richard will not like——"

"Darm his loikes!" ejaculated Genny; "is he to take awa' a girl's character in a breath, without gieing a cause for such a thing? Not if he were twenty baronets.— Coom up!"

"He'll forestall me," muttered Grey.

"Why, you don't think of anything half so foolish, Grey," I said, lowering my voice.

"Ah! but I do."

"This is sheer folly."

"Hasn't he made half Welsdon rail against as good and virtuous a girl as ever breathed."

" He may answer Mr. Genny, but he will not see any sufficient cause to explain to you, I think," I said; " nay more, you will only complicate matters, offend Mercy Ricksworth, and be no nearer your end."

" I have a right, as an honest man, to deliver him a piece of my mind," said Grey; " what do you think I am going to Tramlingford races for ? "

" To keep me company. You and I may never spend a holiday together again, if you think of leaving us three weeks hence for good."

" For good or bad—which, Neider ? "

" For good, to be sure. Yours is a nature that will always find good in the world."

" Well, I hope so. How am I looking ?"

" You're becoming as rosy as the morn again."

" Do you think," in a lower whisper still, " I am learning to forget *her ?* "

" You say you never forget."

"Exactly. If you speak of her twenty years hence, I shall tell you that the romance of my life—my little romance in one chapter—has not died out. I shall be —I almost am now—resigned to the life she has crossed, but I shall always think of her faithfully. Your maxim is that men can shake off such crosses."

"No."

I had begun to think after his fashion, though I did not care to own it then—I knew there was one near me whom I should not readily forget.

"But I shan't fret my way through life, Neider," he said, slapping me suddenly on the knee, with a forced rush of spirits that nearly tilted me out of the trap; "snivelling never did good to mortal, and I won't be one of Genny's 'dead-and-alive lot.' Hurrah for the races! I wish I had a post-horn and a pasteboard nose!"

He cheered up amazingly after this, and exchanged uncomplimentary chaff with the few farmers and villagers proceeding in our direction, and brought a less severe expression to the countenance of Mr. Genny, who laid his thoughts of Sir Richard on the shelf for awhile.

"If this be my last appearance in public, the public shall have no reason to complain of my deficiencies."

"And you'll leave Sir Richard to Genny?"

"Perhaps I will," said he; "and if I do, I'll spend the day looking my gentleman up, till Genny can fix him. Here's the rain leaving off again, and we shall have a jolly day after all. And here's the turn in the road that meets the road from Tramlingford, and all the Tramlingfordians."

"And here's the carriage of Sir Richard Freemantle rattling up behind us," said I.

"By George!—so it is!"

"Ay!—what's that?" said Genny, turning round; "Freemantle's carriage cooming? I'll wait for him here, then, and stroike while the iron's hot. There'll be nothing unpleasant then on the coorse."

" Uncle, you will never be so ridiculous," said Harriet, almost fiercely.

" Ay !" answered Genny, enigmatically.

He drew the dog-cart a little aside, and was proceeding at a slower pace, when the carriage of the Freemantles, with four horses and two post-boys, swirled by at a rapid rate. It was a half-open carriage, containing two ladies and two gentlemen—the lady on our side being the Miss Freemantle who had given me a missive one night to Nicholas Thirsk. The hood of the carriage sheltered Miss Freemantle and her companion from the passing showers; Sir Richard and his friend sat with their backs to the horses, under an umbrella—Sir Richard looking weary, almost miserable. Genny instinctively touched his hat to his landlord, and Sir Richard, with military precision, returned the compliment ; and then the carriage and four were a long way ahead of us, and Mr.

Genny's demands postponed for the present.

"I'll be doon on him yet," muttered Genny, as we turned the bend of the road after the carriage.

"I should have thought Sir Richard's tastes would have led him to eschew horse-racing," I observed to Grey.

"They're tetchy people about here," remarked Grey; "if the great guns of the county stop away, there are fifty people to take offence at it, not to mention the 'Tramlingford Scarifier;' to avoid this Sir Richard brings his death's-head and cross-bones to the gathering. I was here last year, and he sat in a corner of the Grand Stand fast asleep, whilst the cup was run for—he's a fishy being, and a rare dull life his sister must have of it."

"She looked dull enough, poor thing!"

"Poor thing!—with goodness knows how much money waiting for her in the Tramlingford Bank, when she comes of age!" cried Grey.

" She may be pitied for all that."

" Well, she may if you like—I have no
objection. And here's the glorious water-
works again. Look out, Mr. Genny!"

" Ay! lad."

And extra wrappers were on, and the
chaise umbrella re-erected, before the heavy
sheets of rain came down again ; it was in
this fashion, and under these damp circumstances, we drove on to Tramlingford race-
course. Mr. Genny was an economic man,
and objected to Grand Stands; he paid a
shilling or eighteen pence for the horse and
trap to pass into an inner space by the side
of the course—they did not exact Derby
prices in that part of Merry England—
and the horse was placed in charge of a
black-haired, gipsy-looking scamp, and the
trap wedged amongst the chaises, and
broughams, and carts already there.

Mr. Genny and Mr. Grey were shaking
hands with half-a-dozen farmers from the
Welsdon neighbourhood in an instant, and

Harriet sat under the chaise umbrella, pale, and thoughtful, and cold.

"I fear you are not likely to receive much enjoyment this miserable day, Miss Genny," I said.

"I did not expect to enjoy myself, Mr. Neider," said she; "but it was a promise, and you would not relieve me from it."

"Miss Genny, I would have relieved you from it in an instant, had I known—had I thought——"

"Yes," she interrupted, "I am aware of that, but—but my uncle was anxious I should avail myself of this general holiday."

"I am afraid you will get wet here."

"Oh! no, I am well wrapped up."

"You must come into the Stand—this is no place for you."

"I am quite content where I am," she said, with the faintest flash of her past acerbity. I was pleased to hear it, as I should have been to have heard one of her rare musical laughs—it was like the old times coming back again !

"Am I not to be trusted now ? " I said.

" I would trust you with my life, Mr. Neider," she said, "if there were a necessity for bestowing upon you so important a charge. But I would prefer to keep of one party, and I think my uncle would also prefer to remain where he is."

I did not press the point—something in her voice told me how firm she would be if I persisted. I was standing on the moist turf, looking up at the sky, and trying to imagine it was coming down less fast, when she suddenly said :—

" I shall want you to do me a favour, Mr. Neider."

" Willingly," I said with eagerness.

"I am desirous of forestalling my uncle with Sir Richard Freemantle. If any questions are to be asked, and answers expected, I may be the better able to put the first and procure the last—and

Mercy is my cousin, in whom I take an interest. Will you look round the course presently, and let me know whether Sir Richard is keeping to his carriage, and where the carriage is situated?"

" I will go now."

" Thank you."

I set forth alone, after getting on to the race-course, where there were a few promenaders, as defiant of the elements as myself. The prospect that lay before me did not conduce to any great degree of exhilaration—the day was unpropitious, and the rain fell heavily. It was the Derby day seen through a di-minishing glass, and under adverse circum-stances. There was a busy crowd of bet-ting men in the open space before the rickety, draughty wooden building termed the Grand Stand, and these men gave life and animation to the scene, by shouting under their umbrellas their two's and three's to one on the favourites or against the favou-rites of the day, and hanging over the

palings in earnest confabulation with soft
countrymen, who listened to their seductive
voices, accepted their bets, and paid over
*their* stakes, with a faith in human nature,
and in the honesty of betting men, wonderful to witness. There were one or two refreshment booths and gingerbread stalls at
the back of the stand, filled with people standing up for the rain; and there were some
thimble-riggers doing a very bad business
with their confederates, and endeavouring
vainly to lure the British public into the
wet, by the seeming ease with which they
lost their money. Boys and dogs were
plentiful; countrymen in smock frocks,
and countrymen's wives in their Sunday
best,—"tucked, oh! ever so high,"—splashed
and paddled about the wet grass, and did
their best to enjoy themselves in the face of
an adverse fate.

I had no difficulty in discovering the
whereabouts of Sir Richard Freemantle
—there were only three carriages with

attendant post-boys on the course, and Sir Richard's was at the back of the Grand Stand, and unoccupied. Making use of a race-glass of Grey's, I had not much trouble to discover Sir Richard and his party on the first floor of the Grand Stand; they were all gazing ruefully at the damp world beneath them, and at the post in front, from which a cracked bell began at that moment dolefully to ring.

The first race was coming off, and the rural constabulary,—shivering young men in white trowsers, and with shiny capes much too small for them,—mustered in force to clear the course and make themselves generally useful. Turning to retrace my steps, I ran against Peter Ricksworth, who was standing immediately behind me, gaping up at the Grand Stand.

"Would you mind lending me your spy-glass for a moment, Mr. Neider?"

"Certainly not, Mr. Ricksworth."

"I shan't run away with it, or pawn it and

raise money on it, or pass it on to a friend, and swear you never lent it to me," said he, taking the race-glass I proffered him ; " I am an honest man, and bear the best of characters. Thankee."

He turned the race-glass the reverse way, and looked through it at the stand, reversed it again, and cursed it for being misty, and then all manner of colours; finally fixing the focus to his satisfaction, stood glaring through the glass with great apparent interest, until one of the constabulary touched him on the shoulder, and reminded him politely that the course was being cleared, and the first race coming off directly.

Ricksworth turned round with a formidable scowl.

" Can't a man admire the pick o' the company without you stepping in to worry, jackanapes ? "

" Now, Ricksworth, my man, get off the course."

" *Your* man be damned !" said Ricksworth ; " I'm not your man."

"You were once," said the constable, with
a grin.

" Ah ! and a rare broken head or two
there was to make me—I owe you one for
your share in it to this day, Joe Barclay."

" Come, get off the course."

" Can't *me* and my friend stand here a
moment without your jaw?" cried the iras-
cible Peter; "how do you know we don't
belong to the Grand Stand ?"

"Go in it, then, and look sharp !"

" I found a couple of sovereigns in an old
chaney tea-pot this morning, and can afford
to swell it, if I loike. Don't you think I
haven't money to play the bloater, because I have !"

" Clear the course—clear the course !"

" Will you oblige me with my glass,
Ricksworth ?" I suggested.

"Let'shaveanothersquint through it first,"
he said; " where's that ugly white-faced

devil, that robbed my darter of her good name? I'd give my yellow boys to have him by his throat."

"Clear the course!"

"Hould yer jaw, Joe Barclay, or I'll crack it for you."

"CLEAR THE COURSE!" roared Joe, laying his white-gloved hand on Ricksworth's shoulder. Ricksworth struck at it savagely with the opera-glass, and turned round with the face of a demon.

"Hollo, Peter!—if you ride rusty, you'll be in Tramlingford Gaol to night—so move on."

"I'll see you——"

"Ricksworth, are you mad or drunk?" I shouted; "give me the glass, and go your way quietly."

"It's good advice, and I'll take it for once," said Ricksworth, thrusting the opera-glass into my hands and striding towards the opposite side of the course, where the people were collecting. I found my way, with some difficulty, to the Genny equipage, where, to my surprise, a tall, round-shouldered being, in a cut-away plaid coat and white hat, had been added to the party.

The heavy showers had abated by this time, and there was only a steady natural rain now, which soaked one through gradually, and afforded no hopes of clearing up. The rain streamed from the points of the new-comer's umbrella on to his plaid trowsers.

"Here be Mr. Neider," said Genny, "the gentleman I was speaking of just now. Mr. Neider, this is my nephew, Mr. Robin Genny."

And in Mr. Robin Genny I recognized the gentleman, who had walked back with Thirsk to the Haycock Inn, in the early times before the days of farming. I had leisure to study him, after he had shaken hands with me in a very friendly manner— to see, for the first time in my life, a real author in the flesh.

He was a man who had worked hard, and had seen a great deal of life—there was no mistaking those sunken eyes and high cheek bones, that waxen countenance, and the "score" that Time had run up thereon in innumerable fine lines. It was the face of one who had aged before his time; study, fast-living, and a weak constitution, separately, would not have given such a look—together it was natural enough. It was a face that changed its expression very suddenly—at one moment it was an intellectual face, at another a gloomy one, in a third it wore a mocking, reckless air, that reminded me of Thirsk—and there was a fourth expression, a gay, laughing, and frank one, which on that holiday occasion, and in defiance of the rain, was chiefly predominant.

He was standing in the trap, under the chaise umbrella, and hoped he was not depriving me of my place, which he was, though I begged him not to disturb himself, which he did not. He had been cut-

ting some slips of card up, for an amateur
sweep-stake at one shilling per member,
and Mr. Genny had subscribed thereto with
some reluctance, having to pay for himself
and his niece also. He was in excellent
spirits, and anxious to bet Mr. Grey, or
anyone that might feel inclined, any
amount on certain horses, whose names he
had ticked off on the race-card.

"Ye be as free and as foolish with your
mooney as ever, Robin," commented Genny.

"It's only a little amusement, suitable to
time and place, uncle," said his nephew,
laughing; "and I've been in luck's way
lately, and earned lots of the 'needful.'"

"Keep it for the time when you'll stray
out of the road, Robin," said Harriet.

"Never again" he said, quite earnestly.

I fancied that Harriet changed colour, as
she replied,

"You have said that half-a-dozen times
before."

"Ah! but the world was against me then,

now it is saying what a clever fellow I am.
I am clear of the rut, and have struck
out a new path for myself."

" I think I have heard that before, also."

" What an excellent memory you have,
Harriet!"

" I have cause to remember."

She said it bitterly, I fancied, but it did
not appear to convey that impression to
Robin Genny, who laughed as at a pleasant
jest with which she had favoured him.

" You will see there is such a thing as a
new leaf in the life of a reprobate cousin,"
said he; " I have run down to Welsdon to tell
you all about it. I came here first, where
I guessed I should pick up Uncle Matthew,
although I little thought of seeing your
pretty grave self. There, don't look so
fierce at the remarks of an old friend,
Harriet, or I shall begin to wonder what
has happened to you."

He spoke as if he had a right to wonder
—as if he knew her so thoroughly and well,

that that manner of hers, so habitual to me, was something new and strange, and calculated to alarm him with its singularity.

The bell opposite the Grand Stand began to ring again—there was a cry of "They're off!" a general lowering of umbrellas, a rush by of half-a-dozen race-horses and jockeys, a crowd of people breaking into the course, and Farmer Genny the winner of five shillings.

"Lucky in big and little things, uncle," said his nephew, "and the money always turning in the right direction."

"Ay," returned Genny—"it's roight for me, at least."

And he pocketed his five shillings with evident satisfaction.

A few minutes afterwards Mr. Robin Genny and his uncle strolled down the course to see the winner, leaving Mr. Grey and me in attendance on Harriet. Mr. Grey standing moodily under his umbrella, against the shafts of the chaise, gave Harriet the oppor-

tunity to ask, in a low voice, if I had discovered Sir Richard Freemantle.

"Yes, he is in the Grand Stand."

"He will be on the race-course, presently," said Harriet, "and will meet my
uncle, who, in his hasty moods, may peril
his connection with the baronet, and not
attain his own ends. Do you mind coming
with me?—I am tired of sitting here."

"It rains as fast as ever."

"I am not afraid of the rain."

"I wish you would take shelter in the
Grand Stand, Miss Genny."

"Thank you. I have already said 'No'
twice to that."

I knew who had put the question a second
time, but I did not care to mention his
name just then.

"Mr. Grey, will you tell my uncle I shall
be back in a few minutes."

"Certainly," said Grey, with a jump;
"but—but you'll find the grass very
wet."

"My double soles will resist it," she replied.

We left Grey looking doubtfully after us, and entering the course we went on with the stream of people towards the Grand Stand.

I was very glad it rained—there was only one umbrella to share, and she had to take my arm to obtain her fair portion. I was glad to be her confidant in the little matter of Mercy Ricksworth's character, concerning which she was naturally interested. It was a new relation in which I stood to her, and I felt more happy in my mind, and less inclined to see everything in the world under the same neutral tint.

"A hasty word of Mr. Genny's—and you know how hasty he can be—might bring a notice to quit from Sir Richard," said Harriet to me; "if I could but tell uncle half-an-hour hence that I have seen the baronet."

"Sir Richard will think it a strange time

to be addressed on the topic of a servant's character, I fear."

" He has acted strangely."

The course in the neighbourhood of the Grand Stand was well thronged—for so rainy a day the natives of the place, and the nomadic tribes, who let not a horse-race escape them, had now mustered in fair force. The betting men were hanging over the fence again, eloquent, and husky, and persuasive, and the greed of gain drew many a hard-earned sovereign from scantily-filled pockets.

The noise and confusion appeared to alarm Harriet, whose arm I could feel press mine more closely.

" This is my first and last appearance on such a scene," she said, with a little shudder ; " is there no escaping this crowd ? "

" Not if we wish to discover Sir Richard?"

" Look round with your glass, then."

I did so, turning almost instinctively to

the spot where I had seen Sir Richard last. To my own surprise, he was in the same place, and alone. The first floor had become almost empty of its inmates, and he sat shivering where I had last seen him, with the fur collar of his cloak turned up above his ears, and with the most rueful expression on his countenance.

" There's an opportunity of speaking to him now," said she; "I think I will venture after all. Will you wait for me here, Mr. Neider ? "

" No."

She regarded me with surprise.

" I will accompany you. The faces about this Stand and enclosure are not such as I should care for you to meet alone."

" You are considerate," she said ; " but I am not afraid of them."

" And you'll pardon me, but a lady alone in such a place naturally attracts undue attention. I shall go with you."

"This will be an expensive freak of yours, Mr. Neider."

"Not very."

I paid the fee of five shillings each for admission — there were no guinea admission charges to these small country race-stands—and Harriet was for stopping and repaying me on the spot.

"Miss Genny, time is valuable."

"I shall not allow you to ——"

"Miss Genny, you will not lose a chance, now, of giving me pain!"

She coloured, looked angry, and then hastened on again, without replying. We passed through the crowd of betting men to the stand, and up a shaky wooden staircase, to the large breezy room with its open windows, through which the rain and wind came swooping, and out of which one or two idlers were staring.

"It's a strange time," whispered Harriet, as we stood at the door of the room; "but he may return to London to-night, and I—I think I have a right to speak."

"Shall I wait here for you?"

"Yes, I think ——"

Before she could finish the sentence, Sir Richard Freemantle stood face to face with us.

"Will you allow me to pass, please—I ——"

He stopped and glanced from my face to my companion's. A stiff inclination of his head towards me, a raising of his hat to Harriet Genny, and then a movement to descend the stairs.

"One moment, Sir Richard," cried Harriet; "I have come hither in search of you. You will allow me to detain you for an instant."

Sir Richard bowed and remained stationary.

"I have chosen an inopportune moment to address you, Sir Richard," said she; "but it is the only one available. I wish to speak concerning my cousin Mercy."

He looked bewildered for an instant.

"Ah! yes; I had forgotten the relationship, Miss Genny. To be sure, your cousin."

She had made a movement to withdraw apart, but Sir Richard did not move; and, on my attempt to leave them together, he said, very quickly,

"Mr. Neider, you need not leave Miss Genny. I have no secret to communicate—I have nothing to say concerning Mercy Ricksworth."

"She left you at a moment's notice, and you refuse to state the reasons for so harsh a measure, sir!" cried Harriet, indignantly.

"She has not stated those reasons?" Sir Richard asked, with some anxiety.

"She has not."

"Neither can I, Miss Genny," he replied, austerely; "I gave her my word to that effect, and I am not inclined to break it."

"Do you know what it is to rob a poor girl of her character—to refuse all explanation? Have you ever thought of what the consequences may be, sir?"

"She deceived me—that is all I can say."

"That is not sufficient. As her relative, I have a right to demand a fair statement of the case."

"Not if she wish otherwise."

"Sir!" cried Harriet, warmly; "you are playing the part of a coward."

Sir Richard seemed to stand on tiptoe at this charge, but he turned red, and looked a trifle embarrassed.

"Miss Genny," he said, after a painful pause, "I have no more to say, but— good morning!"

"I shall not let it end thus, sir!" cried

Harriet after him, as he descended the stairs, looking nervously at her over his shoulder.

"You are disappointed, Miss Genny," I said.

"Yes—let us return."

When we were on the race-course again she added—

"I shall have gained one point, if I can find my uncle, and tell him that it is vain to seek an explanation. To-morrow, if Sir Richard be at the Hall, I will see his sister Agatha."

Woman proposes!

# CHAPTER XIV.

## HOW THE DAY ENDED.

IT rained all that day on Tramlingford
race-course. An aggravating rain, that gave
promise of leaving off half-a-dozen times,
and then came down the faster, as though to
wash away the delusion. A bad day for
most trades that day on the heath, umbrellas in the way of business, and umbrel-
la-less people inclined to keep under canvas
tents — so long as those tents remained
waterproof—and stand there in defiance of
all opposition, with their backs to the goods
which they hid from the general public.
The thimble-riggers and card-sharpers gave

it up and took to drinking; peripatetic
tradesfolk hawked their goods about in
vain; a man with an ingenious revolving
index-hand, that stopped at various colours,
and encouraged the world to divers wagers,
spun round the hand in vain, and anathe-
matized the weather and the three money-
less urchins who were never tired of watching his operations; the betting men caught
in the aggregate more colds than dupes, and
the jockeys crept about in waterproof ha-
biliments, till the bell rang them and their
horses to the business of the day. Only
the drinking-tents prospered, with the ex-
ception of one man who had speculated in
umbrellas, and gone home early in the afternoon raving mad with delight.

I had long since grown tired of horse-
racing under difficulties, and wondered
when a return to Follingay Farm would be
judged expedient on the part of Mr. Genny.
Harriet sat coiled under the chaise umbrella,
with the great rug spread over her knees,

shivering, and cold, and miserable. Genny, his nephew, Mr. Grey, and even myself, tried, like our contemporaries, to believe we rather liked it.

"We maun see the crack race," said Mr. Genny, his teeth coming in like a castanet accompaniment; "but it be horribly wet!"

"Or passably damp," said his nephew, who had been smoking cigar after cigar, with a rapidity that had long since distanced me.

"I wish some one would make a start, if only for example sake," said Grey aside to me; "I believe if one of these wise folk would have the moral courage to move, we should almost clear the course. Hallo, Ipps, what is it?"

"What time maun ye be going, Mr. Genny?" said he, with a touch of the hat; "'cause I'll see after the grey mare."

"Presently, Ipps. How is she—dry?"

"Wull, pretty dry, sir, considering."

As he passed I felt him touch me on the

arm, and, looking after him, I saw that he turned his head and beckoned me. I followed him to the backs of the various vehicles for some distance, until he stopped suddenly.

"I'm tould I can trust you, sir," he said, looking wistfully at me.

"Trust me with what?"

"With not making a bother aboot me to the ould gent."

The old gent was Mr. Genny, who was at least twenty years his junior.

"Why should I make a bother about you?" said I; "has anything happened to the mare?"

"Noa, sir," and his shrewd little eyes twinkled in his head.

"Well—what is it?"

"A gentleman wants to see you, sir, at the back of the Grand Stand."

"Whom do you mean?—Mr. Thirsk?"

"To be sure, Measter Neider. Oh! but you're quick!"

" *You* knew he was coming here to-day ?"

" I had a suspicion loike, sir."

" You're too old a man to play so false a game, I should have thought, Ipps."

" False be a hard word, Measter Neider."

" How long have you been with Genny ?"

" Nigh on seven-and-thirty year."

" And a traitor to him at the last ! For shame, Ipps—you dishonour him, and your own grey hairs."

" Wull, wull, I was caught in a net, and *he* woond it roond me, and tempted me with his mooney—me who wor a poor man. And he wor only in love, you see."

" You poisoned Genny's dog, Ipps !"

" Lord, forgie me !—how did ye speer that, now ? And, for the Lord's sake, don't tell on to the measter ! I had gone too far then to go back, and it wor all agin tide, and too strong for me. I *can* trust you ?"

And he looked eagerly into my face.

" He is the stanchest fellow under the

sun, Ipps," said a voice close to my ear,
and a moment afterwards the hand of Nicholas Thirsk was extended towards me.

"You are here then!" I said, shaking
hands with him.

"Or my Fetch—guess which!"

It might have been his Fetch, so ghost-
like and colourless was he; only the
touch of his hand was feverish—and the
hands of a Fetch were of ice, I had been
given to understand on good authority.

"You look as if you didn't expect me,
Neider," he said.

"I doubted it, certainly."

"Yet I pledged my word for the second
day of the races—and I'm a man who holds
fast to it."

"Well, are you well?—and has the world
of London smiled more favourably than the
world of Welsdon in the Woods?"

"Would I have given up one world,
before I was sure of a better reception in
the other?" he rejoined.

" There *is* sometimes a slip between the cup and the lip !"

" True, moralist," he answered.  " Ipps, you can go."

" To the old place ?"

" Yes; and keep a sharp look-out, for the life of you."

" All roight !"

Ipps departed, and I said,

" I am sorry Ipps is your head spy and informant, Thirsk."

" A clever workman uses all sorts of tools," replied Thirsk, conceitedly.

" He is an old man, with but spare time before him for repentance."

" Why, you are always thinking of repentance !" cried Thirsk ; " and what is the repentance of that old fellow to me ?  I have not led him into temptation—merely paid him for letting me know when the coast was clear once or twice.  He's a sharp old fellow, though he did think I slept at the back of the house once, and flung half the gravel path up at William Grey's window. And then he was so horribly honest at first, and I hate poor people with too many virtues. And so—amen!"

"And now to change the subject. What do you think of the races?"

"I haven't thought about them yet. The Tramlingford cup is run for next, I believe?"

"Yes."

"The grand race, when the soddened loobies and boobies of the county will be all eyes on a half score of silk jackets— when behind the scenes here a murder might be committed, and no one the wiser."

Thirsk's face flushed, and his dark eyes glittered at me. I could see his small ungloved hand opening and shutting with his excitement.

"Thirsk—you mean something!"

"Patience, and let me shuffle the cards again, before I let you know what the turn-up is.    Come and have some brandy, *mon ami!*"

"No, thank you."

"Keep the cold out and the spirits up! Murder's a-doing, Neider, and I want you to help me!"

"I shan't try to guess at your riddles— when will you please to explain?"

"I repeat, patience."

He linked his arm through mine, and led me through a maze of vans and carts, and horse-tents, until we passed into a refreshment booth, standing a little apart from the general assembly, and driving a fair trade with coachmen, beggars, gipsies, and ostlers.

As we entered, a man advanced and spoke to Thirsk, who whispered a few words in reply, and put some money into his hand. Standing at the bar, Thirsk ordered two glasses of neat brandy, drank his own off at one gulp, and surveyed me with his old mocking look when I diluted mine with some water from a pewter can on the counter.

Thirsk was very much excited—as he set his glass down, it clattered with the agitation of the hand that held it.

"How long before the great race, *now?*" he said to me.

"The bell is ringing, I think."

"So it is!"

The ostlers, coachmen, and nondescripts made a rush from the tent, even the landlord left his business in charge of a dirty servant-maid, tucked up the bottoms of his trowsers from the wet grass, and hurried across to the race-course.

"Didn't I say murder might be done here?"

"And it is to be done," I said, half jestingly, "or you'd never look so pale."

"Am I a white-livered wretch when the time comes to strike a blow?" he said; "courage! — that's not like Nicholas Thirsk!"

He took a purse from his pocket, and

drew therefrom five sovereigns, which he placed in my hand.

"An old debt!" he said.

"Received with thanks," I replied.

"Part of it I can't repay—when I owned I was poor, and you didn't shrink away from me—I can't repay that good feeling. *That*," clapping his hand on my shoulder, "made me your friend till the death."

"Thank you."

"Don't you know, old sceptic, that you are a good fellow, and that there are few of your stock in the world? You've a hard, dry way of showing your likings, but you're honest and true, and I bow," here he made a grave salaam, "to the virtues I have not, and yet envy. You were a mother's boy, and I was a father's bugbear—lo! the difference in *us* is easily accounted for."

"And the secret?"

"Shall speak for itself—come with me."

We left the tent, and turned still more out of the general track, to the high road, where a closed carriage and pair were drawn, as much as possible, under a huge elm tree, that sprung from the opposite side of the hedge, and shaded the road-way. The man who had spoken to Thirsk stood at the horses' heads.

"This looks romantic—eh, Neider?"

"Thirsk, you don't mean to run away with Agatha Freemantle?"

"But I do!"

"You will be discovered."

"I think not," said he, coolly; "I have arranged an odd conglomerated plan of carriage, and railway and carriage again, that will baffle the very devil himself if he set off in pursuit."

"I hope you have well considered all this—it is a step for life."

"For the golden, roseate life lying beyond the present—yes."

"For the life which, shorn of its romance, may be more barren than you think, and may break more hearts than yours.

Oh ! Thirsk, this girl's heart must be worth the prizing to make this sacrifice for you."

"Shan't I prize it? Am I the villain of this love-story ? "

"I hope not—I will believe not."

"In the new life you shall meet me, and judge for yourself. Don't preach at me now—I can't bear it."

He drew the loose cloak he wore more tightly round him, and marched up and down the high road. His face was a troubled one, and I could fancy, watching him, that he was mistrusting his own future. Surely the life he spoke of could not be so bright and roseate to cast such shadows on him in that hour!

The man suddenly mounted to the coach-box, and arrested Thirsk's meditations.

"It's all right, governor."

Thirsk, with a "wait here, please," to me, darted back the way we had come. The race-bell rang out again — the hoarse murmur of the crowd told of the strugglers

for the Tramlingford cup having started
pell-mell for the winning-post—even the
man on the box stood on tiptoe and gaped
after the scurrying dots of men and horses
that flitted across the landscape.

" ' Gipsy Jane ' will win after all, sir," he
called to me from his post of observation;
" the wet's done good for *her* backers."

I murmured an inarticulate response; my
whole interest was absorbed by three
comers — Thirsk and two females — who
were rapidly advancing.

"Nicholas, who is this?" I heard one
agitated voice inquire.

" My friend — one we can trust—Mr.
Neider."

" Was it necessary? "

" I promised you to start without a debt
in the world, and I owed him five pounds.
And I wished him here, dearest, to give us
God speed on our way."

They were close upon me; the female on
the left of Miss Freemantle kept her face·

studiously concealed from me. Miss Freemantle trembled very much and looked anxiously, almost piteously, towards me.

"You are the friend of him I choose
before all the world, Mr. Neider. Will you
be the first to blame me for this step?" she
asked, in a faint voice.

"It is scarcely a wise one," I could but
answer.

"It is not a hasty one, believe me. I
have weighed every chance, and every probability, and the whole world is against me
and my Nicholas. I trust my future with
him fearlessly."

"I will wish every happiness for that
future, Miss Freemantle."

"Thank you."

She entered the carriage and began to
cry passionately, almost childishly; her
female companion endeavouring by some
earnest words to soothe her.

"Thirsk, she is but a girl still," I said;
"have you acted well or generously?"

"Could I have acted in any other manner?" he asked, almost fiercely.

"Why did you bring me here as a witness—almost as a confederate?" I said.

"A friend's face is worth seeing at the last—and I would not have *her* think me quite friendless, or that all the world was to turn against her from this act. Wish her happiness again, and say a word to cheer her up a little. She is moved like the wind by a word."

He almost pushed me towards the carriage door, standing at which I reiterated my best wishes for her happiness. I could not think, on the spur of the moment, of any reassuring words—I saw only rashness and folly in the step that took her from her natural protector. She had lived in an atmosphere of romance which she had created for herself, and knew little of life and the harsh realities before her. Her companion shrank back once more, but I had already recognized Mercy Ricksworth.

"I am glad you are not going away un-accompanied, Miss Freemantle."

"I take a faithful friend with me," and she pressed Mercy's hand in hers; "a girl who has suffered much for my sake."

"Can I deliver any message at home, Miss Mercy?" I inquired.

"No!—no!—I shall write to-morrow. Mr. Thirsk," she cried, "are we not losing valuable time?"

"Right, Mercy—the wisest head on the youngest pair of shoulders. Let us be on the wing!"

He sprang into the carriage, whence he reached his hand towards me.

"Say, God speed, if you even object to this bold stroke for a wife."

"God speed you!"

"Amen. God speed us! And now, coach-man, drive like the devil!"

The carriage whirled away, and I was standing alone in the Queen's highway. A few moments, and the carriage was a blot in the distance, rendered indistinct and misty by the heavy slanting rain. A strange flitting away, at a strange time, under circumstances that told of much strategy and plotting—of an ill reward for many years of guardianship, honest and well meant, if severe.

Still, God speed the plotter who had gained his ends, and the trusting woman who had placed her future in his hands—I could but wish them that.

And yet, amidst it all, I could but doubt it!

*      *      *      *      *

Returning thoughtfully to the race-course, I met a jostling crowd of men and children, and bedraggled women, talking, whooping and screaming, and in the middle thereof honest Peter Ricksworth in the grasp of three of the rural constabulary, who found quite sufficient work to hold him, drunk as he was.

The crowd swept past me, and I caught at the ragged fringe of it, in the shape of a bullet-headed youth of fourteen.

"What's the matter?"

"A row in the Grand Stand—he got in somehow, and tried to knock Sir Richard Freemantle head-over-heels, sir—and jumped on his hat, sir, and such a jolly kick up there was as ever you seed in your life, sir! He got into the Stand with somebody else's ticket, they say, sir," added this communicative youth.

Almost involuntarily, I felt for the pass I had purchased at an earlier period of the day.

It was missing.

END OF THE SECOND BOOK.

# BOOK III.

## Old Promises.

"In love and in debt and in drink this many and many a year."

BROME.

"*Cleander.* But tell me, I pray this, Pasiphilo, whome dost thou thinke Polynesta liketh better, Erastrato or me?"

GASCOIGNE.

# CHAPTER I.

## AFTER THE SHOCK.

" ELOPEMENT IN HIGH LIFE!" What a glorious subject for a county paper, when Parliament has adjourned, operas have closed, and the assizes haven't commenced! What a deal can be made of a sensation piece of news in the hands of a careful sub-editor. Wonderful perversion of dashes and initials, like a *chronique scandaleuse* of the Town and Country Magazine times— glorious halo of mystery, through which may peer the star of promise of full revelations in the next number. An elopement in high life!—an event that does not happen

every day, and affords matter for discussion
and pleasant jest amongst respectable fami·
lies whose members have behaved themselves properly, and thank God are not
as other mortals—romantic and weak, and
easily tempted, and rash ! It was all as well
known in the county two days after the
elopement, as who had won the Tramling·
ford Cup for that year of grace, 1856.
And Sir Richard Freemantle shut himself
in his library at the Hall, and was not at
home to those kind friends and acquaint·
ances who came to console him—and learn
the latest news.

Mr. Genny looked across the breakfast-
table at his nephew, who was favouring
him with his company for a week or two,
and said—

" That be your friend !"

This was four days after the races, when
the marriage of Nicholas Thirsk with
Agatha Freemantle had been duly chroni-
cled in the daily papers.

"And a very shrewd friend too—don't you think so, uncle?"

"Ay, in his way," was the dry response.

"Besides, it was a love-match, and Sir Richard played the haughty tyrant, and sought to mar the happiness of the young couple—why, it's a story that should soften the heart of a mill-stone."

"I begin to see why he laid oot forty pounds in learning the farming," said Genny; "and ye sent him here with your recommendations to deceive me, ye rascal!"

His nephew laughed.

"That's an effort I should never be fool-hardy enough to attempt. Why, I put forty pounds into your pocket."

"Ay—and added five years to my loife. Ye moight as well have sent me a deevil's imp."

"All's fair in love or in war—eh, Harriet?"

"No—I think not."

"I appeal to Mr. Neider."

"'When we know the true story, we shall be better able to judge what is fair."

"And so subject postponed, *sine die*," cried Genny the younger.

He turned the conversation with an ease and readiness that evinced no small degree of tact, and presently he was discoursing upon books, and literary men and literary matters—a topic that fascinated me, for it spoke of a world that I had turned from, and despaired of entering.

Robin Genny was a man who won upon me, but whose traits of character did not display themselves too readily. He was a quick talker, and knew a little of everything, and spoke of everything in a way and manner that had its attraction, and never failed to gain listeners. A good-tempered, easy fellow enough, probably—fond of idling time away, and assuredly not a hard worker; he spoke of pressing work on hand, and the dunning letters of publishers, and yet never set pen

to paper during his first four days' stay
with us, but lounged about the farm in his
plaid suit, with his hands in his trowser's
pockets.

" How do you like farming ? " he said to
me, at a later hour.

" Pretty well."

" My cousin Harriet tells me you once
had a fancy for scribbling. Lucky you
dropped it—for it's hard lines, and don't
pay."

I was vexed that Harriet had mentioned
my old *penchant* to him, but I believe
I did not betray my vexation.

" If you are one of the tip-tops it is all
very well," said he ; " but I'm not a tip-top
—I'm a utility man."

" May I ask what that is ? "

" One who works on newspapers — slaves
at the proof-sheets of dunces who pay for
their abortions to see the light, and cuts
them up afterwards in the magazines and
papers wherein he may have the honour

to be principal butcher—a man who trans-
lates, or cabbages, or does anything for cash
in hand."

" Do you write novels ? "

" Oh ! no," with a shudder, " I have
enough to read them—novels are not my
*forte.*  I think I shall try a fast one some day,
if I can obtain a fair price for the article.
Or a sensation one, with a good ghost or
two.  Do you know of a good ghost,
now ? "

I looked at him, but Robin Genny was
perfectly serious, or had an enviable power
of repressing his real thoughts.   He
munched at a straw in his mouth, and
dawdled on at my side through the farm-yard.

" Literature is purely business with you?"

"Purely business," replied he, carelessly—
" once, of course, it was romance, and a
dream of a laurel wreath as big as a
Covent Garden basket of greens.   Now
there isn't a dozen men out of my set who
have ever heard of Robin Genny—and,

when I was a 'young un' I thought of making the world ring."

I almost fancied that he sighed over the old ambitions he had had.

" I *did* try my hand at a novel once," I confessed.

" What became of it? "

" I burned it in the kitchen range of Follingay Farm."

" What was it about? "

" Oh! the usual elements of a novel—love, and jealousy, and misconstruction, and all clearing away at the end of Vol. III. in a grand tableau."

" Ah! you did well not to publish it, Neider," said he; " it must have fallen into the hands of the twentieth-rate publishers—those who would have offered you one price and paid you another, and trusted to your natural objection to law not to press the matter. Men who swindle authors out of a copyright with their eyes open, and get their living by the brains of men more trustworthy and honourable than themselves. Better no author at all than a tool in such hands."

" Are there such sharks in the profession ? "

" Oh ! yes—firms that will speculate in anything, *for a conshideration*, from an illustrated bible to a half-penny magazine—that work in the dark, and put names a trifle more respectable than their own on the title-page, *for a conshideration* too. But they find me a great deal of work—why should I carp at my employers ? "

" Why don't you give them up ?"

" Well !" with a drawl, " I'm up to their shabby tricks, and they can't do me any harm. And one man's money is as good as another's, you see; and as they don't swindle me now, why should I care how others are swindled ? If my profession would turn virtuously indignant at the wrongs done to its class, I'd give an honest kick with the rest; but I can't go kicking all alone, and making myself conspicuous. Besides, I have an idea that a few sharp-shooters like these do a certain amount of good, and keep us lively and looking after our own interests. And so it's all right, I daresay."

And he chose a fresh straw, with the fresh subject that he started immediately. He was a practical man, who looked at every thing in a pounds, shillings and pence light; who had outlived romance and fancy, and took things as he found them, and was not Quixotic enough to attempt reformation. He earned money and spent money, and lived a tolerably easy life; was well known to the trade as a clever writer, and to his class as a good-tempered, jolly fellow, who would lend a crown out of his last ten shillings, and never remind an unfortunate Bohemian of the little account owing. He would not discourse on literary matters again that day, and I was anxious to hear more concerning them. How he made his first step in life, and when the barriers were surmounted, and who first took him by the hand, and praised his work and set his heart beating and his eyes swimming with tears.  But he would not talk of his early days, when he was a "young un;" he feigned to have forgotten them, and to consider them days to be laughed at and satirized, as if an author ever forgot his first work, and the first word that cheered him on, and the first chop that that savage critic gave him over the fingers!

"Let us go back to the Farm and have some of my old uncle's home-brewed," said he; "we've talked of the shop till I'm dusty."

"What was the first success you ever made, now?"

"Oh! I'll tell you to-morrow."

Putting off till to-morrow had been Robin Genny's habit through life, although I was not aware of it then.

Returning towards the Farm he said—

" That's a stiff piece of goods staring at us over the fence there—who's the party?"

I looked in the direction indicated.

" Sir Richard Freemantle; why, he's beckoning me!"

" I will wish you good morning, then."

And Robin Genny went on his way, and left me to approach the baronet.

Sir Richard Freemantle was leaning over the plantation fence that divided his grounds from Mr. Genny's; a very pale, stern face it was that met my own as I advanced.

" Do you mind stepping over this fence for a few moments, Mr. Neider?"

The next instant, I was at the baronet's side.

" I have been watching for you the last two hours," he said, leading the way into the depths of the plantation.

" Indeed!"

" I did not care to arouse general curiosity by calling at the Farm, though I should have done so had I not seen you in

the course of the morning. Mr. Neider,"
turning round and facing me suddenly,
" have you heard from your friend yet?"

" Mr. Thirsk?"

" The same."

" I received a newspaper this morning,
addressed in his handwriting, and containing the advertisement of his marriage."

" Nothing more ?"

" Nothing more, sir."

" I had a hope that he would write to
you and say something about himself and—
and wife."

I could but regret that I had not heard
from Nicholas Thirsk, and I ventured to
express a hope that Sir Richard had received a letter from his sister.

"I have not," he said, closing his thin
lips together. " I am not worth a line,
even soliciting that forgiveness which I
shall be too ready to grant."

" I am rejoiced to hear that, sir ! " I cried.

" Why are *you* rejoiced, Mr. Neider?"

and the dreamy grey eyes assumed a sudden keenness for which I had not hitherto given them credit.

"I think such news would be gratefully received by your sister."

"And Nicholas Thirsk?" he added.

I hesitated in my reply. Words that Thirsk had uttered in excited moments told of a deep vindictive feeling against the man who stood before me. And yet Thirsk had gained his ends, the man was baffled, and the successful schemer need bear malice no longer.

"I should think he would be pleased to forget the by-gones, and begin a new life, wherein you and *he* might judge each other more temperately and justly."

"I am afraid you know but little of your friend."

"I have not attempted to fathom his character, Sir Richard, but I have been a witness to many efforts of a generous nature to assert itself."

"Efforts that have always failed, Mr. Neider."

"I will not say always."

"You made his acquaintance at Welsdon?"

"Yes, sir."

"Ah! you are a friend of a few months. I have studied his character for years."

"And were mistaken in it, sir—he has told me that story."

"Well, well, it is a story that belongs to the past—who was right, or who was wrong in it, we will not consider now. Surely the present is bitter enough, and lonely enough for me!"

"It may soon brighten, sir."

"I will try and believe it;" and he began raking the dead leaves at our feet with his stick, as he had raked amongst the ruins of Welsdon Castle in my first conversation with him.

After a silence of some duration, he said, looking up suddenly—

"Don't you think I bear my disappointment like a philosopher?"

"I have not had much opportunity of judging, Sir Richard," I replied.

"I bear no malice—I take the news of her want of confidence, and of my loss, as I would take the news of her death. I am very sorry, but I am striving hard for resignation."

"It may be a happy match, after all."

"I should like to be her friend still," he said; "perhaps when you write to Mr. Thirsk you will say you met me accidentally, and that I implied as much?"

"I will, sir."

"Thank you—it will be a favour conferred."

He raked over the leaves at his feet again, and traced sundry strange characters in the damp mould beneath them.

"Would you take me now for a very hard man?" he asked suddenly.

I could scarcely forbear a smile.

"Speak frankly—you have seen me before, and must have formed some impression."

" My first impression was that you were a stern man, Sir Richard—living much in the past, and studying it too much."

" And forgetting the present and my duties in it ? " he added.

" Partly."

" And your second impression, if you had one ? "

" That it was only your manner—a bad habit of repressing emotion and evincing no sympathy, the better to sustain the character you have adopted, or have deemed most fitting."

" I don't say you are right—I can't expect you to read me very correctly, Mr. Neider," said he ; " but, good heavens !—you are nearer the truth than my half-sister, my ward, has been all her life ! She could see only the calm exterior, and never the heart playing beneath. I was not the twaddling, or the loving brother of the foolish novels she read—so I was the man of stone, who loved nothing, and whom nothing could love. I tried to be the foil to her own impulsiveness, and over-acted my part, and helped to bring about this evil. But I acted for the best, and my heart acquits me. You might imply this, too, indirectly?" he said, with an upward glance at me again.

"At the first opportunity it will be a pleasant task, Sir Richard."

"I should act it over again," said he, candidly; "a few features softened here and there—the result of this experience— but still the past offered me back, I should betray the whole trust of her father and mine, to act otherwise. You need not mention this, though."

"Certainly not."

"I do not believe she will write to me— it is not likely—and as I am the aggrieved person, I cannot make the first advances," said he, with his old haughtiness; "but if your friend correspond with you, it is in

your hands, sir, to promote much happiness.
If they have resolved to spurn my friendship,
why, I have lived within myself some twenty
years, and can afford to bide the time when
they will seek me out. I am not a demonstrative man, and a little contents me. How
is Miss Genny?"

"She is very well, thank you."

"You may tell her I am perfectly willing
to offer her a full explanation *now*," said he,
with the ghost of a smile playing over his
thin lips.

"I think Miss Genny is able to guess all
now, sir."

"It is very probable. It is the first
edition of the same story, and Mercy Ricksworth was too excitable, and betrayed the
plans of her for whom she professes so much
affection. I thought I had been on my
guard for life after that deliberate attempt
to deceive me—but, there—there—there—it
is all past and gone, and there's the future
to look forward to—eh, Mr. Neider?"

"Wherein everybody must understand each other better, Sir Richard. It appears to me to have been hitherto a life of mistakes."

"Have *you* never been greatly mistaken?"

"I fear so."

"It is a peculiar sensation—good morning, Mr. Neider."

"Good morning, Sir Richard."

I had proceeded a few steps in the direction of the farm-land, when he came after me.

"If you should hear from Mr. Thirsk, you might—ahem!—think of me. I am a very hard man in reality, Mr. Neider—cold, and inflexible, and unsympathizing, but I—I should like to hear if she be well."

"I will inform you of any news which Mr. Thirsk may feel inclined to communicate, Sir Richard."

"Thank you."

He extended his hand towards me—a thin, cold hand, that lay in mine like a dead fish for a moment, and then was withdrawn. We re-echoed our good mornings and parted—he to his home, which a disappointment had scathed; I to the Farm, where a great trial awaited me.

# CHAPTER II.

## A FRIEND THE LESS.

I HAD no occasion to communicate with Sir Richard Freemantle. Nicholas Thirsk did not favour me with any particulars concerning the progress of his marriage felicity. Probably he had started on his honeymoon, and might not be in England. Having attained his object, and succeeded in the one great scheme of his life, he could afford to forget his friends—even the scenes and characters of the past estate he had abjured.

"He was always a slap-dash fellow," said Robin Genny to me one day, when Thirsk was the subject of our conversation; "you need not be surprised that he has not written—he always hated trouble of all kinds. Pity he has no concentrativeness," added he, as if all the concentrativeness in the world had fallen to his own particular share.

" His better chances in life will make a better man of him."

" I'm not quite so certain that more money will improve him. I have known him with his pockets full of money; and a rare fellow he was to stand treat whilst he had it, and a rare fund of humour had he in the merry days before he tried the Mephistopheles vein! He wrote an article once for a magazine of ours, and, by George! it was the best thing, in its way, the public had had for a long while. When he was offered terms for a series of articles, he wrote back that it was like anyone's hanged impertinence—he didn't call it hanged exactly—to take him for a writing fellow.

That's Nicholas Thirsk sober—did you ever see him drunk?"

"No."

"A man possessed with seven devils might be a match for him. Very strange you have never seen him drunk; I suppose there wasn't much chance at Follingay Farm?"

"He had turned over a new leaf, and fallen into better company."

"Humph—is that personal?"

"Oh, no—I don't suppose you were Nicholas Thirsk's tempter."

"He was a tempter of me, though, the young scamp! Many an honest pound have I lost in that gentleman's society. And many a day's work spoiled by a splitting headache after the enjoyment thereof. Oh! they were rare days, though!—and all work and no play will make dull boys of the best of us! I wonder what would become of me, too, if I hadn't this safety-valve of country quarters. By

George, it's a grand change for a man!"

"You work hard sometimes."

"I believe you—forty-eight hours at a stretch, occasionally. You should see the pile of work I have promised to knock through by Christmas!"

"Shall you finish it by Christmas?"

"Yes—thereabouts. I ought to be working here, but there are so many things to distract one's attention. Farming life, farm-pupils, fresh air, a general kind of laziness over the establishment at this time of year—and Harriet."

I winced at the last inducement to forego work, and he winced too at my change of colour, and twitched at his long brown moustache. His cousin's name had escaped him, and he proceeded to enlarge upon it for my edification.

"Not that she hasn't been my incentive to work many a time—real, downright hard work, that brought in almost money enough to pay my debts. If she only knew what a pile of work there is in my portmanteau!"

She guessed it, however, for the following day she asked him whether he intended to idle all his time away; and spoke so much about the folly of wasting it, that that very afternoon he sat down to the little table before the farm-house window, and began writing at a railroad pace. Grey and I sat and watched the rapid progress of his pen over the paper, and wondered what he could be writing about, for his thoughts to flow so easily. Constant practice had rendered his pen a ready one, and it was with perhaps a pang of enviable feeling that I regarded his performance, and contrasted it with the lot I had chosen for myself.

And yet my enviable feeling was really not for his advantages, his tact in writing, or that quasi genius which kept his head above water—I chose to think so, but I had more than a mere suspicion that I was jealous of him, and of Harriet's power over him.

For I could see that Harriet exerted a strange influence — that he respected her sound common sense — and that every day seemed to add to his interest in her, and to the earnest looks with which he regarded her. Remembering William Grey's words to me one day concerning him, I still had not fairly set him down as a lover of Harriet Genny's. He was her cousin, and naturally friendly in his manner to her, but he betrayed no excitement or embarrassment, or timidity in her presence, till the first week of his stay there was drawing to a close. Then his character seemed to change, or some old character that I had not known to be resumed, and Harriet grew strangely petulant and capricious, and undecided in her manners.

I sought information from William Grey; he was the one least likely to suspect any change in me, and I drew him out concerning Robin Genny's former visits, and his general style of address to Harriet.

"About the same as usual," said Grey. "He has only been here twice before during my stay—was a regular creep-mouse fellow for the first few days—all round shoulders and trowsers pockets—a *blasé* being, whom nothing seemed possible to brighten. Then he took a turn, or received a talking from Harriet, on the sly, for he went to work like a steam-engine, and took to Harriet the more for scolding him, and fell quite into a loving track, if you understand what that means."

"And she ?"

"Oh, good-tempered and bad-tempered, by fits and starts, just as she always is," said Grey, surveying me intently.

"Just as she always is—she is not always so! If it were not for some hidden care, anxiety, secret, what you will, that is weighing her down, Grey, she'd be a very different girl."

"She's a good girl—a warm-hearted, feel-

K 2

ing girl, I own that, Neider.  Don't fire up so!"

"I haven't fired up."

"But you have——and ah! old fellow, your turn has come to put your head in the trap!" he cried; "will you confess, now?"

"I have nothing to confess, Grey."

He looked disappointed.

"Perhaps you are right," he said, after a few moment's silence; "it is not everyone who is fool enough to prate of the girl he is inclined to fall in love with, and of the hopes and sorrows born from his passion. You're a chap who can keep his secret to himself.  I'm of a different nature, and inclined to bawl it forth into the ears of the first friend I take to.  I can't expect to be your confidant, Neider."

"If there were anything really serious to tell, Grey," I said, hesitating; "if there were a story worth telling!"

"Some other time when there is," said

he. "Did I inform you I was going away next week?"

"Certainly not."

"Finally settled, Alf — the world before me, and old Welsdon to be nothing more than a painful reminiscence."

"All painful?"

"Well, I won't say that. I think," with a wistful look towards me, "that I found a true friend here—and that's something as times go. Do you remember our talk about a farm on the joint-stock principle, with your mother for housekeeper—eh?"

"To be sure."

"If you marry and settle, there's an end of it—if the Fates go against you, some of these days I'll step into your lonely farm, amongst the Cumberland mountains, sit down before your fireside and make you an honest man's offer. I'll cheer you up, Neider, and turn you out a bright and presentable being. Don't forget this."

"You're the most unselfish of men."

"There may be more self in it than you bargain for—by the way, you did not tell me, Neider, you saw *her* on the race day."

"It was hardly fair to declare it—it was Thirsk's secret, not mine. How did you ascertain it?"

"From old Ricksworth."

"He's in prison."

"Oh, no, he's not. He was fined five pounds for the assault, and I paid it."

"Rather foolish, wasn't it?"

"Rather, perhaps," said Grey; "but she *is* fond of the old scamp. He was very grateful for the trouble I had taken, and prison would only have made him a worse father to *her*."

"He has been in prison before?"

"So he has—and you can see how it has damaged his morals."

Perceiving me laugh at this, he broke forth into his own good-tempered laugh in return, and we went downstairs to the farm-parlour, in better spirits than we had retired thence.

The week passed in watching Robin Genny —studying him—trying to discover further traits of his character. But he was hard at work that week; all the morning and afternoon he wrote in the deserted farm parlour, at his favourite place under the window—and steadily, rapidly, the sheets of MS. seemed to grow under his hand. On our return from the fields, he would put away his work, and take a share in the general conversation, or in the games at cards which his uncle was inclined to introduce now the nights were lengthening, or in the spirits which were placed on the table every evening whilst Robin Genny remained a guest.

The last night of William Grey's stay there was quite a little feast for the occasion, and decanters of wine added to the spirits, and a cake made, and the farm servants called in to drink William Grey's health, and wish him a fair life's journey. He had been a tractable pupil, partial to farming, and a favourite of Genny's—and Genny did his best to show he would be missed at Welsdon.

"Persevering and industrious, and regular in your habits, and no fool—ye'll make the best of farmers, Mr. Grey," said Genny.

"Thank you for your opinion."

"And here's my best wishes, and long loife to ye, sir!" cried Genny, drinking his health for the third time; "ye're a credit to my teaching."

"That's all right, then," said Grey, laughing.

"And we'll make a braw noight of it for once," said Genny; "and Harriet shall gie us some songs on the piano—and Robin and she shall try some of their old duets together—eh, Robin?"

"I'll do my best. Harriet, do you remember any of our old songs?"

"It is two years since I attempted them, Robin."

"We'll try them for the good of the

company, and go back two years, then."

"Impossible!" cried Harriet, and there was a meaning in her voice that brought the blood to Robin Genny's face. I saw it there, and my heart thrilled again.

It was an evening intended to be festive; but the majority of us were sad; the piano was out of tune, Robin Genny forgot every one of his duets, and cracked horribly in all the upper notes, and even lost a little of his good temper over his repeated failures; he made up with copious libations of gin and water, however, till Harriet said a few words in a low tone, and checked his habit of grasping too often at the decanter.

"Doan't stay your cousin," cried Genny, who was in high spirits, genuine home-spun farmer's spirits, and had seen the last bit of by-play; "we'll send my gentleman to bed to-night as jolly as a trooper. It bean't the first toime Robin Genny has not known the stairs from the banisters."

"Robin thinks of rising early, uncle, and finishing his work."

"So I do," cried Robin.

"And so you will," said Harriet.

"To be sure. See what influence this stern little Spartan has over a man."

"Will you be silent!" urged Harriet, with a frown.

Robin Genny spoke not a word more.

That night Grey left us. He and I rode over in Mr. Genny's chaise to the railroad station. He wished to catch the last train —the same train as that by which Nicholas Thirsk had left some little while ago. What a different parting, and what a different friend to shake hands with and say ' Good-bye !

Grey was a sensitive, simple-hearted fellow, and could scarcely keep the tears back. His voice was a strange compound of the natural and the unnatural, the falsetto and

the bass profondo. His hand was the grip
of a vice.

"Good-bye, my dear Neider; don't forget me."

"Trust me."

"And—and if you are not in love with
Harriet Genny now, but are likely to be,
I would look sharp. Delays are dangerous,
you know."

"Grey, I love her!" I said, in a hoarse
whisper.

"I'm sorry."

"Confession for confession, you see.
And now, what are you sorry for?"

"I don't know. I don't wish to dash
your hopes down," said he; "but try and
learn the best or worst at once, before Robin
Genny goes away. And take care! Good-
bye."

He had just time to leap into the train,
and leave me comparing his warning with
that last one of Nicholas Thirsk's, which
had showed Thirsk was the shrewder man,

and took more heed of things passing around him.

The same warning, and of no avail to me!

# CHAPTER III.

## THE GREAT PLUNGE.

I THOUGHT of Robin Genny all the way home. Midst the natural sorrow at parting with one I could believe a stanch friend, Robin Genny would intrude, take the foremost place, and gradually set aside all other thoughts. Was he my rival, or was he merely Harriet Genny's cousin, dreaming not of a nearer and dearer tie of relationship?

Yet she had told me not to think of her; had, with a touch of terror in her voice, prayed that no word or look of hers had set me dreaming of that which was impossible; had spoken indirectly of some

mysterious barrier—perhaps her own an-
tipathy!—that must irrevocably part us.
That she spoke hurriedly, without a moment's thought, was not assuring, and that
her demeanour towards me had been
changed from that day, was more a bad sign
than a good one.

I drove home, brooding on all this, with
the warnings of my late co-pupils faintly
sounding in my ears; I entered the farm-
yard, more of a lover than I had ever been.

Ipps awaited me.

" A foine night, Measter Neider."

" Yes."

" So we've lost another on 'em."

" Yes."

" Mayhap I maun be all the better for it,
now," he muttered—" for eighty odd years
an honest man, sir."

" Take the horse round to the stable."

" You'll keep it all from the measter—I
think you guv me your word on the
coorse."

" Yes."

" I should loike the measter allus to think me a fair servant, though I be going, you must know."

" Going ?"

" Yes—I guved warning to-noight. I can't. stop and face him, and I wor offered another place loike. And he wor too good a measter to turn agin. I shan't die a happy mon."

" In whose service are you about to enter ?"

" I haven't mentioned it to the measter —you mayhap guess."

" Mr. Thirsk's ?"

" Roight, sir."

" You're an old man to think of a change in life."

" I'm unsettled loike !" he cried, excitedly, —" I've become a sneak, and a pisoner, and a thief. And I was such a light-hearted chap !"

" A thief too ?"

"Wull, you *dropped* your pass to the Grand Stand, and I gave it to Peter Ricksworth. He made a row just at the time we wanted it, though he worn't in our confidence, of course. All bluster and no brains —it wouldn't ha' done to trust him."

There was a strange mixture of conceit in his superior craft, and shame at the part he had played, amidst the old man's discourse; but he was a traitor to the homestead, and I had lost all interest in him.

"Where is the master?"

"He's gone to bed, and left the young couple coorting——"

"Left them *what?*"

"Love-making, I am incloined to think."

And Ipps looked sly.

I left him to take the horse and chaise to the stables, turned the handle of the outer door, entered the passage, and locked and bolted the door on the inside, with a noisy demonstrativeness, which I intended as a warning of my approach.

But they were talking earnestly, almost passionately, and had forgotten me. As I neared the door of " the best room," I could but hear the subject of discourse, and pause without, and even listen, like a traitor.

For a few moments to stand there listening, with my temples throbbing, and my heart making fitful plunges, and my demented thoughts striving to excuse the part I played there. Was it not concerning me, and was it not my happiness that was affected by their strange discourse? To know that she loved Robin Genny was to save her from much painful persecution on my own part; and if I could but learn it in those unworthy moments spent there!

" This is the insane folly of two years ago," I heard her say; " the passion without root—the spur of the moment, which would deceive me, and has ever deceived yourself."

" Have you lost all confidence in me, Harriet ? "

" Have you deserved that I should retain any?" was the cold reply; " year after year this same profession of attachment, followed by the same forgetfulness."

" Never forgetfulness."

" Let us be simply common friends from this night—I see no good, no love, no honour to follow that which you propose. Oh! Robin, I ask you to give back——"

" Harriet, I will give back nothing! You have ever misjudged me; you are mistaken in me now. You will make no allowance for my struggles in the world around me. Let us end this folly of an age, and share all together—we have wasted many years."

" No, no, no!"

" Harriet, have you forgotten the past ?"

"The dream of a foolish girl."

"The promise made to one who loved us both, and died believing in us. Think."

"My God! bear me witness how it is a thought that has been ever before me!"

"Then have faith in me. I, who have done nothing to forget it, demand it standing here."

"You demand it with a brain dizzy with drink!" she cried, indignantly.

"Harriet!" he cried.

"Don't come near me—I believe it. Speak of the promise to-morrow, and ask the fulfilment of my share in it, and I will keep my word."

"I will ask it."

Harriet was speaking again, but I stole noiselessly away. I had heard enough to crush out every hope of mine, and I was dying for fresh air— for the cool night air upon my fevered temples — for the quiet stars to look down upon my trouble—for the silent commune with my own heart, which I distrusted still.

I unfastened the door again, crossed the farm-yard, and went out on the country road, to think of this, and act all this, and strive to see beyond, and what would come of it. I did not know how fast a hold she had upon my heart till then, for until then I had not wholly despaired.

The farm-house dog, Nero, who had been let loose by Ipps for the night, offered himself as companion; he had acknowledged me as one of the family some time since, and occasionally favoured me with his company. But his noisy barking disturbed me, and I sent him back to his place of watch, and went on alone, at a rapid pace, as far as the Castle ruins, where I turned back and retraced my steps. I scarcely know if I thought at all—certainly nothing that was rational or could be brought to any sober test. As bewildered and excited I returned to the farm-house, found the door still unfastened—though the clock on the stairs was striking eleven—and walked into the silent room, that I had quitted at an earlier hour with William Grey, and where Harriet and Robin Genny had talked so earnestly and strangely.

A silent but not deserted room, for she was crouched on the floor before the hollow fire; her arms flung over the chair beside her, and her head buried in her arms.

As I advanced into the room, a low moan escaped her.

"Miss Genny," I said, "what is the matter?"

She was on her feet facing me the instant afterwards.

"Nothing, sir."

"You are unhappy—you have been sorely tried this evening, Miss Genny."

"How do you know that?" she asked, suspiciously.

"Pardon me, but I have heard—intentionally heard, for my heart was sorely tried, and I was tempted to my own unhappiness—part of a serious conversation between you and your cousin."

"You are frank, yet false," she answered.

"I am sorry that you think so. My heart was tried, I repeat; if there be no excuse in that, I have none other to offer."

"Tell me what you have heard?" she cried, impatiently.

"You were speaking of some promise in which he had faith, and you had not—you were speaking of a past from which he seemed to urge a claim upon you and your love."

"You have heard all, then?"

The room went whirling round with me, and I lost all self-command, all remembrance of her warning words made on that evening when my heart betrayed me. I saw her passing across the threshold of a life where she would be ever distant and away from me; I felt that she was troubled, and I knew I loved her. It was my one faint chance before the morrow when he was asked to speak again and end all, and I struck for it blindly, rashly, and forgot all else.

"Miss Genny—Harriet—I have heard that which has filled me with a horror which only you can dissipate—only one word of yours to give me hope for all my future life! Don't leave me with that look of indignation,—the offering of a life's devotion is, at least, worthy of an answer."

She paused and turned towards me with a varying countenance—the pride, the fear, softening to a strange pity at my earnestness.

"Mr. Neider, this is romantic folly, and I am too old and worldly for your generous passion. This is——pray let me go."

And she wrung her hands before me as I intercepted her flight towards the door.

"An answer, Miss Genny—I think I have a right to it."

"What can you possibly expect from me?"

"An assertion that I am every way unworthy of you, or that there is a chance —however faint and weak— of making you my wife."

"There is no chance," she murmured.

"You do not love Robin Genny—you dare not own that."

"I dare!" and she looked defiantly into my face.

"Miss Genny, I am answered."

"I have been his promised wife five years—and a few weeks will end all engagements in a happy marriage."

Her voice never rung more mournfully than when she spoke of such a blissful end to all engagements.

"Love, honour, duty, and more than that, compel me to his side—it is my rightful place, and I will take it and fear nothing."

"Does he love you?"

"He says so—he thinks so.   Years ago, when I was touched with that fever of romance from which you suffer now, I thought he loved me too well, and neglected for me too many of his worldly interests. He says he has not changed, and seeks me still, a portionless bride.   Why should I doubt him—what right have I to doubt him?"

"Miss Genny, there is some mystery beyond all this, which you do not care to fathom—something between you and that happiness of which you speak so coldly," I urged; "I see it plainly written on your face."

"You are mistaken," she replied; "more, you are blinded by your folly, and see all things darkly.   Surely you are answered, and will not seek to pain me by idly shifting thus your ground of argument—surely you will let me pass you now?"

The tears were in her eyes, her lip was quivering, her whole demeanour was as that of one struggling to resist an avowal, and be gone from me, ere it leaped to the light and betrayed her. And I could not resist her wish—for I loved her, and she beseeched me with such earnestness.

I stood aside.

"Forgive me, Miss Genny — God bless you, and lead your steps aright! Never more a word to pain you from my lips."

She passed me, and I thought she had gone, when I felt her light hand touch my shoulder.

"Mr. Neider—you, you don't think that —that I expected such a declaration as your own—or that in any way, from curiosity, a woman s vanity, even a woman s love, I sought its utterance ?"

"No," I answered.

"It was a painful story, that I might have told you months ago, and checked all this ; it was on my lips once, and fear, or a natural embarrassment, hindered the avowal. It was a story that seemed burnt into my brain one day, and then lost to me and thrown aside the next."

"Why do you tell me this now?" I cried.

Her eyes met mine, and her face was scarlet for an instant—for one instant, and then she might have risen from her grave, so ghastly white was she.

"They say no woman ever received a confession of love without having encouraged it!—and oh! you will not think that. It will be my bitterest reminiscence if you harbour such a thought!"

"My own folly and wilful blindness, Miss Genny," I replied; "I am justly punished for my vain ambition."

"You will learn to smile at all this some day," she said; "you are young, and I am two years on the wrong side of you, and old enough in thought to be your mother. you will find in the world one so much more fitted to be your wife; so much younger, brighter, fairer than the betrothed of Robin Genny."

It was the consolation that the world

always gives — I had adopted a similar method of solace in William Grey's case—I had heard it, read it fifty times. It might verge on the truth as a rule, but in that hour there was no comfort to be gained from all the wise men of that world wherein I was promised so much.

She stole away silently, almost reluctantly —as though a footfall might startle the consolation she had never left with me— and I sank into the chair she had abandoned, and pressed my burning temples with my hands, and looked at the ashes in the grate, as though they had been the path of life that stretched before me from that cruel day.

# CHAPTER IV.

## THE LOVERS.

Robin Genny was at work early on the following day.  Descending into the farm-parlour at an early hour, I was surprised to find him so soon at his post by the window.

He looked up as I entered, and said " Good morning."

" Good morning, Mr. Genny—I am not interrupting you, I hope?"

" Good company never stands in the way of my work," he replied.  " I write at all times, and in all places, save in a study, which is my abomination—being such a dull place. I'm not in your way here, Mr. Neider?"

"Oh! no," I answered; "I am going over the land."

"I wish I could go with you," he said, with a glance at his MS.; "I have a horrible headache, that the fresh air might cure."

"Are you very busy?"

"Well, I am. Time and magazine-day wait for no man, so I'll keep my headache in all its intentness. Have you seen my cousin Harriet this morning?"

I had not seen his cousin Harriet, and as he recommenced writing immediately after my reply, I passed into the farm-yard. Crossing the window at which he sat, I saw that the pen had fallen from his hand, and he was staring very dreamily across the room —thinking of the cousin for whom he was waiting there, I felt assured.

And that cousin—would she tell Robin Genny of my last night's proposal, of all that extravagance of action into which my

heart had betrayed me—or would it ever remain a secret between her and me, that we
should carry to our graves? Something un-
real, and romantic, and foolish, which could
not intrude into the garish outer world and
live. Something that had flashed across
her path and startled her, and vanished—
lighting up for a moment a new mystery,
of which she had never dreamed till
then.

I did little service to Mr. Genny that
morning. Whether the men were in the
fields fulfilling their allotted tasks, or there
were five horse or fifty in the meadows, or
the new plough acted well, or had even
arrived, I was as ignorant as though I had
kept to the room wherein I had fought for
sleep and failed.

Never was my occupation more of a
name and a sham; never felt I more how
hard, prosaic, and unprofitable was the calling I had adopted. In the first shock of a
great disappointment, all callings must feel

alike, all ambitions beyond the one that has died at our feet feel scarcely worth the thought of a moment. I did not consider so in that hour; I delivered my hearty curse on farming life in general, and then drifted away to thoughts of her who had turned me from my track.

Thoughts of the re-engagement between her and Robin Genny, and why it had lasted so long, and with such little happiness to her. Of her strange, fretful moods, which were, I knew, foreign to her natural character, and seemed an evidence of inward torture and uncertainty—a shrinking away from the future, which lay dark and impenetrable before her. Of my gradual study of those varied moods, and the errors into which those studies led me—the vain belief that a noble spirit fretted against the monotony and unsympathy of her present life, and pined for an existence wherein might be more of affection, and kindred feeling and interest. Of the stern truths which followed all this, and dismayed me, and beat me from the path whereon was sunlight for myself; versed me in the bitter knowledge that it was Robin Genny's love she had pined for, and which, doubting, had rendered her unsettled, and her true character unguessed at. And yet they hovered near me, confusing everything, those other thoughts which had rendered me a dreamer, and set me in an evanescent world—thoughts of her brighter moods, her fairer words and looks, her approximation to a happiness that awakened mine, and in which Robin Genny had no life, and seemed forgotten.

And so the old thoughts and the new, and the end of all no nearer certainty.

I was in the farm-house parlour again; the maid-servants were arranging the breakfast-table—Robin Genny still wrote as if for his life; his uncle stood with his back to the fire, watching his nephew's movements with no little wonderment. Harriet Genny was not visible.

"It be the oddest way of arning money I ever knew in my loife," said the farmer to me as I entered. "I doan't think I could arn a brass farthing at it myself. Where be the people that buys such scrawl now?"

"Oh! over there," muttered his nephew, absently.

"Maun hard work it must be," said he, "to be always sitting about and thinking of something worth printing—or not worth printing," he added, drily; "and going at it noight and morning, morning and noight, and never dreaming of fresh air."

"We don't work quite so hard, uncle."

"Ye doan't, I'll wager!" said his uncle, with a twinkling of his keen eyes towards me.

"I get through plenty of work too," cried his aggrieved nephew, from the corner.

"Ay, but ye do it in jumps somehow—a week's skulk, and then a week's solitary confinement, and always unsettled. Bean't that it?"

" No."

" Wull, ye know best."

Harriet entered shortly after this brief dialogue, a shade more pale, possibly a shade more firm and grave. I observed that Robin Genny turned to her with a nervous, vacillating glance as she entered, and that her first looks were for the student at the window.

" You are busy, Robin ? "

" Yes. I have resolved to finish this by twelve o'clock. It has been long promised, and I'm working at it like a steam-engine. Adieu to the easy life of the past, and welcome to the life in earnest lying before me."

" Hollo, young man !" cried his uncle, " didn't ye sleep well last noight ? "

" I don't know—I don't think I did."

" Ye're talking like a play-actor, and play-actors always talk nonsense."

" On the stage—they're solid matter-of-fact fellows off."

" Ay. Perhaps they be."

A miserable morning following that breakfast. I remember that all its brightness changed, that the rain fell heavily, and hindered out-door work, and left little for me to do save to feign reading by the fireside, and to watch Robin Genny over the leaves of my book. He was my rival, and I could not keep my eyes from him. He had known Harriet Genny years before me, and had fallen naturally in love and served five years 'for her—and now his reward was coming, a blessing ever to thank God for !

Had the thought of the nearness of his happiness made a different man of him? It was a different face on which the grey light of the clouded sky fell; it was like his promised life, tinged with the earnestness that was new to him. There was intelligence thereon, and a certain faith in the future. I could fancy he had made himself a host of promises since yesterday, and had sworn to keep them, for the sake of her who committed her happiness to his charge; that he had awakened to the realities of life, and the necessity there was to regard life's duties in a different manner. He had been an idler on the banks perhaps, and now he leaped into the stream and struck out manfully.

Still, most men have these sudden thoughts of reformation, and many sink back to their past estate, tiring of those persistent efforts which alone can lead to the sphere beyond their own. Was Robin Genny one to fight the battle manfully, or would he flinch in the heat of the conflict, and let braver men push by him? I was not sufficiently acquainted with his character to guess, but I had gathered sufficient news of him to fear.

Watching him more intently, I was reminded of Mr. Genny's rough estimate of his labours that morning, and could fancy that that morning's work might be an epitome of his life's. He certainly wrote by fits and starts, as though one train of thoughts was foreign to a second, and there was a jostling between them that stopped the pen, and turned him from his occupation. But that he worked at all evinced no common power of concentration; surely he had much to trouble and distract him, standing on the verge of the new life, concerning which he had spoken so confidently that day. And he worked hard, though fitfully; and if his pen stopped, and he looked beyond at all that lay before him, there was a bright figure to gaze at, that might well lure him from his task. Now and then he glanced towards the old-fashioned time-piece on the mantel-shelf, and set to his task afresh, working more vigorously as the time sped on. The last hour his gaze never wandered, nor did his pen swerve from the paper, and as twelve struck he cried—

"'*Un fait accompli*,' Neider! Pooh, I

never worked so hard in my life. I said that it should be done, though; and who says I never keep my word?"

I felt that Harriet had said it once, and he had resented it, and been anxious to disprove the charge against him. Had said it yesternight, before I stole into the passage, and learned from eavesdropping the folly of the hopes I had fostered!

When she re-entered the room he cried—

"I have finished it, Harriet! What now?"

"What now?" she repeated—almost gasped.

"What new charge against my habits, my weakness of mind, the instability that loses all the prizes? Come!"

"I make no charge."

"From the night to the morning is but a change of purpose in me. Words spoken by one 'dizzy with drink' are forgotten in the sober daylight. I remind you

of my wishes last night—of your own promises concerning them."

He held his hand towards her—both his
hands, which shook a little with his energy
—and she slowly advanced and placed hers
within them.   My jealous eyes were watching them, and they thought of me as some
statue in the room that had no feeling,
sympathy, or comprehension.    And she,—
how pale she was, how steadily she looked
at him, how strangely "Robin" sounded
from her lips!

Genny, still holding her hands, turned to
me with a beaming countenance.

"Neider, will you wish two old sweet-
hearts joy?   We are going to be married
in three weeks."

"With all my heart!—with all my heart!"

I started up, and let the book fall to the
ground.  I saw her colour change at my vain
effort at composure, as I reeled rather than
walked from the room.

# CHAPTER V.

## A SKETCH OF THE PAST.

"Mr. Neider, the rain has cleared off; shall we have a stroll towards the town? I must look up the stationery department."

"I have no objection."

It was the afternoon of the same day, and Robin Genny was the first speaker. A few hours since the lovers had acknowledged their future intentions, and I had left them to themselves.

When the author and I were on the road he said—

"Mr. Neider, I am going to compliment you on your taste."

" Indeed !"

" Harriet has told me that you asked her once to be your wife."

" Right."

I answered hoarsely, and with a spasmodic contraction of my fingers, but he did not notice my embarrassment.  He even laughed ; having won the battle he could afford to laugh, according to the general rule.

"She's a girl who keeps nothing back," he cried, with more enthusiasm than I had hitherto seen him exhibit; "frank and open as the day.  Perhaps a little too frank, sometimes," he added more gravely, as an unpleasant reminiscence appeared to suggest itself.

" You are not indignant at my entering the lists against you, Mr. Genny."

" My dear Neider "—he had become quite familiar lately—" how did you know I was in the lists, when I was a little in doubt myself."

"Ha!" and I turned upon him for an explanation, as though I had a right to ask it.

"Possibly not in doubt," he corrected, "but still plodding on in the old mill-horse style, and forgetting in my work half my thoughts of the one waiting for me in this dull old spot. And yet hardly forgetting," he corrected a second time; "a sort of—sort of——."

"Indifference," I added, seeing that he was at a loss for a word.

"Confound it, no!" he cried; "sins enough at my door, without the shame of indifference. More like over-certainty, when one is sure of a thing, and so lets it not trouble him and interfere with his duties. I don't know that there is a word for it—and if there is, I can't fix it. Does it matter?"

"Not much."

"I can put my ideas better in shape on a sheet of paper, Neider—take my paper away, and I'm floored. But hang it, what made you think of such a thundering bad word as indifference?"

"I really don't know."

"You're not jealous, now, of my success with Harriet?" said he; "it was a success before your time, and so there was not a fair chance for you. And as I'm not a jealous man I admire your taste, and am glad to see that there are others in the world capable of distinguishing the real merits of my quiet cousin. Neider," suddenly clapping me on the back, with a heartiness that sent me a few feet in advance of him on the road, "she will make a man of me!"

"Don't you lay claim to the appellative yet?"

"A bachelor's only half a man, and a literary bachelor is an addle-headed being, who is preyed upon by harpies, and becomes a child in their hands. Harriet will fight my tradesmen's battles, pay my tradesmen's bills, keep me to the sticking point when that cursed 're-action' carries me the devil knows where."

" Are you subject to re-action ?"

" I used to be," he said, evasively; "it's a general complaint. You know what all work makes of the fabulous Jack? "

" Yes."

"Dull, the moralist says—I say, desperate. And now comes the time for Robin Genny to regard things practically, and make his cousin an author's wife. Upon my soul, I should have been a better man if she had been my wife two years ago."

" I wish she had."

He laughed again.

" Two years ago I was down here no better or worse off, and there was a long talk between us—almost a quarrel —and she thought I should never make a good husband, or save money, or become domesticated; and she or I, or both parties, mutually consenting, put off the evil or the happy day for a couple more years;

and somehow, after all, I haven't saved twenty pounds. Odd, isn't it?"

" It seems a little odd."

He was a babbler, and forced his confidence upon me. His heart was full, his brain was excited, and he wished to talk of Harriet to me; he had some dreamy, good-natured idea that it was a kind of consolation that he was offering me for my disappointment. A generous rival, whose every word pained me, however, for it betrayed his weakness, and seemed to throw a shadow on *her* future.

" I never could save, you see," he continued—" a man in my position has no one to offer him valuable advice. I ought to have been married long ago—she would have had me at any time—she only wished to see me a little more steady and business-like. And I was a fool, who went on any-how!"

" A sad confession, Genny. But all the folly dies out on the wedding-day."

" Oh ! of course," he said, easily—" if a man don't buckle to with a will, when there's another to provide for, he's a man fit for nothing in this world."

" Yes—and the sooner out of it the better."

" I shall turn a saving man, like Uncle Genny," he continued—" cut all the loose fish of my acquaintance, and cultivate the friendship of the steady ones. You're a steady one."

I laughed, and thanked him for the compliment. He was so communicative, that I ventured to ask him what had brought about the first engagement with his cousin Harriet. The whole story was before me in an instant.

" She was an orphan at an early age, and was brought up with me under my mother's roof. I think my mother must have loved her more than myself, for I was always being lectured on my thoughtlessness, and my impulsiveness, and all the other

'nesses' that mothers will worry their off-
spring about.  She and Harriet were true
mother and child, and Harriet was
grateful for my mother's affection, and
took my part — God bless her! — when
the old lady was too hard upon me, and
had a style of her own, that did far
more good than my mother's.  So the poor
old lady began to think that Harriet was
just fit for me, and the only one to make
my life a blessing, and died believing we
should be man and wife some day.  It was
her happiest thought upon her dying bed;
for we pledged our troth, as fine writers
say, before her, and vowed to be ever true
and faithful, and to take each other for
husband and wife when the fitting time
arrived.  That's the story, Neider—what do
you think of it?"

I did not give my opinion, and in a
moment he had forgotten that he had asked
for it.  I was thinking of promises made at
deathbeds, and all that she had said con-

cerning them, one early day at Follingay
Farm. She had called them cruel exactions
when speaking of mine—did the shadow of
her own press heavily upon her? Had she
outlived her girlish liking for this man at
her side, and never known what love was,
and let gratitude for a second mother
delude her, till the waking came?

He spoke again, and turned my thoughts
a little.

" My mother was a shrewd woman, who
knew what was best for me," said he; "she
pictured this day, and all the comforts it
would bring me, and all the better life in
store for me, guided by Harriet, solaced by
her sympathy, sustained by her rare confidence. Well, I believe it now."

" Did you ever doubt it?" I cried,
hastily.

" No!" he said, taken aback by my im-
petuosity; "but the time sped on after she
had gone to Uncle Genny's home, and
*somehow*"—(it was a favourite word of his

that *somehow*)—" she grew more fidgety
and cross—just a touch of Uncle Genny's
peculiar style—and I couldn't see, like a
fool, that it was my fault or my ways that
were unsettling her, until our long talk
this morning. Why, she would have even
*given me up* to-day, if I had had the least
doubt of my happiness with her—as if
that were likely, Neider."

" It seems impossible."

" And so I'll become the best of husbands—a model creature, that other wives
shall envy—and every promise that I make
her I'll keep, or curse me for a knave next
time you meet me !"

He meant it then at least; his cheeks
were flushed, he seemed to grow more tall
as he walked on beside me; his very look
was noble. I could not fancy him, just
then, the weak-minded, easily-led man he
had confessed himself to be.

I could look at him and doubt again
when we were in the village, and he had

drawn me very quickly and unceremoniously into the Haycock Inn.

"A bottle of the best port wine in your
cellar!" he cried to the landlady's daughter.
"No, stop a moment, while we are about
it, you must drink the health of the happy
couple in the true wine of champagne—it's
a favourite drink when I've cash to spare.
A bottle of Veuve Cliquot's, miss, if there
be such a thing in your cellar."

The landlady's daughter looked per-
plexed at the demand; she did not know
if there were any champagne in stock;
there was not much inquiry for it at
Welsdon in the Woods, but she'd ask her
mother. The mother found us a bottle
of champagne—which was "not even full
brand," said Genny, disparagingly—and my
companion made the counter ring with the
sovereign he flung upon it.

"Will you walk into the best r——"
began the landlady.

"Oh, hang your best rooms!" cried

Genny, unwiring and getting rid of the cork with a celerity that told of much practice. "Where's your glass, Neider? Look out! Now!"

"Here's health and happiness to the future Mr. and Mrs. Genny!"

"'Amen, sings the clerk,'" he said; "and here's Alfred Neider well out of his love troubles, and a fair life before him, with lots of money to spend. And here's utter confusion to all shams—for this is gooseberry vinegar, by God!"

He frowned over the bar at the licensed victuallers for an instant, and then laughed heartily at their amazement, and dropped the change from the sovereign into his pocket, without counting it. I could believe he had been a friend of Nicholas Thirsk's—it was all my absent friend's dash exemplified before me.

"And good luck to the poor!" said a voice; and Peter Ricksworth, who had slouched out of his favourite study, the tap-room, stood behind us with his greedy black eyes fixed on the champagne bottle.

"What, Uncle Peter!" said Genny; "just in time to drink my very good health, too. Another glass, landlady, for a gentleman of distinction."

"She won't believe it!" said Ricksworth, with a grin.

The glass was placed on the counter, and Robin filled, and handed it to his disreputable relative.

"What am I to drink now?" said he, swaying from his heels to his toes in a manner extremely suggestive of too much drink already.

"Good luck!—isn't that comprehensive enough?"

"Good luck, my hearties!" and he tossed the wine off, and made a wry face afterwards.

"Ugh!—that's what you call gentlemen's drink, I suppose?"

"They say so at the 'Haycock,'" was Robin Genny's satirical comment.

"It's rum slush—what's its name?"

"Champagne."

"And I have been drinking champagne like beer, and never knowed it! Champagne, now! Upon my soul, Robin, I should just like to try it again, now you say it is champagne. Ho! ho! ho!" with a roar that made every glass behind the bar ring, "Peter Ricksworth drinking champagne at the 'Haycock!'"

"Hold your glass, reprobate," said his nephew; "and now, how's my good aunt and Mercy?"

"Your good aunt goes it hot and strong in the usual style, young feller. She was over-sarcy last night, so I floored her."

"That's bad news!" cried Genny.

"She went on so, Robin," explained Mr. Ricksworth; "she was so unmerciful with her jaw, Robin, and it was all aginst the goodest, best of girls — because she went away sudden - like, with the mistress she thinks so much of. As if Mercy don't know what is best—as if it wor right to go at her hammer - and - tongs, like a damned steam-ingin—as if I'd stand it!" he bawled, with his face becoming darker and more full of rage at the reminiscence.

"Steady!" said Genny, quietly.

"I shall make a bolt of it, now," said he, in a tone less removed from the danger of bursting something in his head; " I shall give her up, and go to Lunnon!—I won't support an old she-devil like her, and get no thanks for it, and be etarnally preached at! Why don't she swear and bully like a reasonable Christian?—that's what I want to know! What does she come the parson over me for?"

"I shall see you in London, then?" said Robin.

"I'll bet five pounds you will."

"Good day, then."

"You're in a hurry, man," turning on his

nephew with his habitual scowl; "I mind the time when you wouldn't ha' been so ready to shake an uncle off. When you wanted to meet that Thirsty fellow hereabouts, and keep old Genny in the dark."

"I had the pleasure of spending an evening at Welsdon's End then — right you are, Uncle Peter," said he; "and the Thirsty fellow managed well, didn't he?"

He had succeeded in his idea of turning the conversation to a less unpleasant topic, for Peter Ricksworth laughed again vociferously.

"He managed to get a rich wife!" cried Ricksworth, "and play the old sodger with that gallows ugly corpse of a man, whose life I'd care no more for taking than a rabbit's. I owes him a grudge, mind—I owes him a grudge!"

And in his excitement he crushed the wine-glass almost to powder in his hand.

"That's a shilling's-worth of damage," said he; "Mrs. Harrison, I think my nephew won't mind settling that."

Whether Robin Genny had an objection or not, did not appear; he paid the damage, and, anxious to curtail the conversation, led the way from the Inn. But Peter Ricksworth was a man with a grievance, and one seldom escapes the recital of a man's wrongs under such circumstances.

"He turned my gal away—he had turned me away before that; he's an icy devil, with no mercy in him; and if I had got at him on the Stand—Ipps, gave me your ticket—I'd have left him as black as a coal. Oh! he's a grand, bouncing barrownight, that thinks hisself a god-a-mighty of this parish, and makes poor fellows like me go all wrong."

Peter looked the picture of injured innocence after this, and began to whimper and discourse volubly, if hoarsely, on all the afflictions that had beset him since his boyhood. He continued with us till within sight of the farm-house, when he shook hands affectionately, gave us his blessing, and strolled a few paces back with his hands in his pockets. We were not quite rid of him, for an instant afterwards he was at our side again.

"What was that jaw about at the bar, Robin Genny?"

"What is that to you, Peter?"

"About a future Mrs. Genny—Harriet, for a sixpence!"

"Well, you're right. We publish the banns next Sunday, so I need not make a secret of it."

"I'll wish you joy, if you don't get it."

"But I shall get it."

"Are you quite sure?"

"What do you mean by 'quite sure'?" cried Robin, indignantly.

"You always were a bit of a fly-away cove, you know," explained Peter; "going first this way, and then that, and led by the last man's palaver — take a warning from your poor old uncle, Robin. You won't find such a stunning warning anywhere out a penny tract—what the devil the parson will find to preach about when I'm in Lunnon, the Lord knows!"

And reflecting on the future subjects of the Vicar of Welsdon's sermons, Peter-the-black-sheep left us finally for good.

# CHAPTER VI.

## THE MARRIAGE.

"*I publish the banns of marriage between Robin Genny, bachelor, of Westminster, Middlesex, and Harriet Genny, spinster, of this parish.*" Strangely it sounded in the old church of Welsdon, and set my heart beating a little faster, though I held my prayer-book with a firmer grip, lest the trembling of my hands should betray that any fire were lingering yet within me. I was to live all down, and forget it, and seek other ambitions—it had become a world of promises, and that I had promised her!

The announcement of Harriet Genny's

coming marriage took the country folk by surprise, and country folk express their emotions more visibly in rural districts than in towns and cities. There was quite a rustling in the free seats; people stood up unceremoniously and turned their open-mouthed, vacuous-looking countenances towards our pew—even Sir Richard Free-mantle's pale face veered for a moment in our direction — old ladies began whisper-ing together—and one boy of fifteen, attached to the Farm, became so excited about the feet as to kick the hat of that hypocrite Ipps out of the free seats, and half-way down the middle aisle.

I bore it better the second week; I had begun to live down my little romance by that time; to talk it over soberly with my-self, and plainly see the folly of it, and where nursing so vain a delusion might lead me in the end. I was neither a coward nor a madman at that time; I bore my trouble—and it was a greater one than I care to avow here—without alarming my friends by my misanthropic looks or morbid airs. I tried to sink my passion within myself, and work my way on in the world, as though it had never lived ; I believed that I succeeded. What I suffered in the effort need not be paraded in this story—it would be idle vapouring, and from the purpose I have set myself.

A few days before the wedding, Harriet Genny very calmly and quietly mooted the subject of her engagement. She had altered for the better, since the little storm of three weeks ago ; the mind once resolved to a great step in life, shakes off the petty excitabilities that disturb the even tenor of its way.

She had become a different woman; as grave, perhaps, but free from all those little irritable fits, the exhibition of which had puzzled me, perhaps attracted me towards her, in the hope of fathoming a mystery.

" What has Robin Genny told you ?" she asked, with a little of her past abruptness; " I see he has made a friend of you."

"He has told me of the long engagement that existed between you," said I in reply.

" How it began in the old times, when he and I were almost boy and girl?"

" Yes."

"All of the past, and nothing of the future, then ?"

" He spoke of the future—I had forgotten that!"

" May I ask what he said ?"

" He believed the better time was in store for him, solaced by your sympathy, and sustained by your rare confidence—I quote his very words."

"He said that !" she cried, with flushing cheeks.

" More, Miss Genny—he meant that."

" Surely it is not a hard fate to share the battle of life with one so hopeful, to say a kind word in his hour of need, and by sharing his troubles with him make them lighter, and keep his heart from sinking. Would you believe that I am a woman of great patience?"

"I can believe you are a woman with a great loving heart," I answered.

"If we should ever meet again, Mr. Neider, you will find me in a new character —the true character, which I have hidden here, or natural circumstances have thrown a veil across. It is a grand task that lies before me," she added, thoughtfully; "and I will do my duty in it, and make his life a something that has never been, or he has never guessed at. God will reward——"

She stopped and turned hastily away. That was a promise she could not assert or build on; standing on the threshold of the life beyond, she could not bring God's blessing on the efforts to become the best of wives, or make him who claimed her hand the truest, noblest of husbands. I could fancy, looking at her then, that amidst her sanguine view of coming happiness there fell athwart it a doubt of all her efforts and his strength. To see her face change thus, and note the look of pain that rested there, was to pray with her silently for the better times beyond her strange, unfathomable future.

Strange and unfathomable, for I was doubting too; amidst my belief that she had long loved Robin Genny, there would come a suspicion that the marriage was not one of hearts—that the old promise was as a vow that her conscience could not set aside, although her will and common sense rebelled against it. To think of all the past was to strengthen that conviction; but the past I was not dwelling upon then. I had the clue, but it was not my place, and I had not the heart to follow it.

They were married, and went away to

spend the honeymoon. A quiet wedding enough, on a wet day, with little speech-making, and Mr. Genny in bad spirits. No guests invited; no friends of either Robin or Harriet present — it was diffi-cult to say who were their friends, or where they were at that time—Mr. Genny to give the bride away, and I to support the author in the character of groomsman; a little wine to be drunk in the Farm par-lour, and beer *ad libitum* to every man, wo-man, and child on the Follingay estate.

" We shall be always glad to see you at our little town crib," said Robin Genny, shaking me heartily by the hand; "for auld lang syne's sake don't forget us, Mr. Neider."

"Doubtless we shall meet some day. Meanwhile, my best wishes for the lasting happiness of you both !"

"Thank you, old fellow—thank you."

I shook hands with Harriet Genny—Harriet Genny still !—and looked very firm, and grave, and pale—the reflex of the calm, handsome face that met my own, and was going away for ever. Never again, never again to brighten the old farm, and make the place like home to me and that troubled old man, who did not know how much he loved her until the final parting came!

They were gone at last, and we drew our chairs closer to the fire, and looked rather dismally at each other — farmer and pupil.

" Ay, but it looks odd already," said he, with a sigh.

" Somewhat dull. It's the contrast."

" I suppose we shall get used to it," he continued; "just as she, poor lass, will grow used to him, and the ways which she has feared so long."

" Feared—what do you mean ? "

" Ay—what's the matter, lad ? "

" What do you mean by feared ?"

" Well, it's been a fast-and-loose kind

o 2

of engagement for soom years, and Harriet was always in doubt how much he thought or cared for her in Loondon. He seldom wrote—and his was a gay loife, mixing amongst gay men, and letting them make him more worse and oidle than he naturally be. Ay, but he's a rum 'un; and if he doan't make her happy now,—darm me! but this will be a black day for the lot of us!"

" But—but she loves him?"

" Ay," said he, "so she says. I doan't think she knows hardly—for she has been fighting not to think too much aboot it, I'm incloined to think. Oh! but she can be wilful and daring when the fit's on her, loike the rest of an odd lot. Still, I hope she loves him—if she doan't, she'll soon larn. Stir the fire, young chap—how cold it is!"

" It is a frost this afternoon."

" Ay!—ay!—and these early frosts nip at the hearts of things! I hope," with a twitch to his ear, "all my little queer tempers did not make her toired of the Farm at last, and anxious for a splash like. I woan't think that, God bless her! You're sparing the wine, now?"

"Oh! no. Shall I fill your glass?"

"Ay! it passes away the toime. I'm a-thinking," said he, after a long pause, "that ye'd ha' made a decentish sort of husband for my Harriet. Odd to have these thoughts come creeping up one's back, but it's been my idea—though I wouldn't ha' told ye before this, moind—some four or foive months or so. Ye'll be a good farmer."

"You stand alone in your verdict."

"Ay! but I'm roight! Ye mayn't loike it much, but ye're pig-headed, you see, and will grub along decentish—and ye're quiet, and doan't turn away because a thing's hard, or not to your moind. Ye're loike Harriet in some things—and though she's older, you'd ha' suited each other tolerably well. No matter, it wasn't to be, so here's luck to the t'others. I've drunk it once or twice before to-noight, but we can't have too much of a good thing. Ay! but it's very odd without her," he added again.

Matthew Genny, farmer, never became used to the change in my time. Peter Ricksworth look leave of his wife and Welsdon End, and Genny tried the experiment of making Mercy's mother his housekeeper, under proviso that, in the event of Peter's sudden re-appearance, Mrs. Ricksworth should abandon her post.

But Mrs. Ricksworth was not to my taste; and her austere and demonstrative piety— not to mention her icy parlour manners, and her nagging dairy ones—did not add much to the halo of saintship she expected everyone to see round her mob cap. A well-meaning woman, who made the worst of everything, and never indulged in a smile; who would have thrown me into a melancholy mad state, had not I been anxious for out-door walks during her stay.

I left Follingay Farm before my year had expired. I had learned much from Mr. Genny, who was the best of farmers, and to whose practical knowledge I was indebted for all my after-success in that sphere which had been thrust upon me, and to which I was slowly, surely settling down.

"I ha' advertised for a pupil or two," he said to me at parting; "it's getting a little bit too narrow here to breathe freely. And I ha' got used to coompany, ye see. Well, young man, good-bye to ye, ye'll prosper if ye work fairly—and work fairly ye will, for it's in ye! And there's my best wishes into the bargain; and if ye wroite to an old man a loine or two of news, it won't make him feel less lonely, or without friends. God bless ye, my lad, and foind a wife as fast as ye can, and remember me to your mother. Something tells me we aren't saying good-bye for ever."

"To be sure not! You must come and see my Cumberland farm."

" Coomberland land is maun gritty—ye'll do better in some other county."

" Wherever I settle down, I hope to see the face of a friend."

" Thankee, lad.  And ye'll see me then, if ye mean it."

He did not think how I should see him, or what a change awaited him.  Dame Fortune, that had brought him many prizes, and made him tolerably rich, might bring an avalanche upon the Farm with the next turn of her wheel.  Here the prizes, there the blanks, and life a lottery; men and women playing high and cautiously, and the background full of silent, shadowy watchers, perhaps.

In a world of changes, could he, or I, or those whose lives have been faintly reflected in these pages, expect the stream of life ever to flow on eternally peaceful and un-rippled?  Are there not streams dried up by burning suns, and streams that overflow their banks and spread desolation right and left ?   Far away as dream-land, and beyond it, lie the glassy rivers untroubled by the storm, and steeped for ever in undying sunshine !

END OF THE THIRD BOOK.

# BOOK IV.

## After!

"A ring of a rush would tie as much love together as a gammon of gold."

GREENE.

" From trouble when I fastest flie,
Then find I most adversitie."

SIR DAVID LINDSAY.

# CHAPTER I.

## A JOINT-STOCK SPECULATION.

It was home again in the little quiet Cumberland farm. The old home before the days at Welsdon; where I was heart-free and full of fancies, and looked at life so differently! The dear, old farm, that had been my German father's hobby, and wherein he had lost one or two thousand pounds in strange experiments on land, and had only begun to experience the blessing of profits a few months previous to his death. The farm, well managed, would always be a little independence for my mother and me, he had thought, and he prayed me not to abandon it for the sake of that mother, whose protection and comfort I was to be when he was gone. I promised him upon his death-bed, and this was the result— neither unlooked for nor unprofitable. During my absence from Cumberland, the land had been placed under the direction of a farm-bailiff, whose management had been lax, and whose interest was only lukewarm ; it had been a fair season for farmers in general, or the loss at the mountain farm might have been serious. As it was, we were a hundred pounds poorer that year—and the loss was fortunate for me. It braced my energies, dissipated all gloomy thoughts, sank the past recollections and the vain ambitions, and turned me with a full, but willing, heart to the pursuits I had chosen. I worked hard, and, thanks to Mr. Genny's past tuition, was able to see progress before my own harvest had been gathered. in. A fair harvest all over the country that year, and less of the insufferable mountain rains that rendered farming in the Cumberland valleys always a dangerous speculation.

It was a contrast to my old life in the same spot; a little while since, and I was wandering about the mountain passes, and idling by the tarns, dreaming of the fame that was not to descend upon me, and the name in the midst of men that was never to be mine. Now all the poet's fancies, and the manuscripts that had borne no fruit, were gone, and I regretted them not. I worked at the restoration of my mother's mountain home; for the fair, full-hearted mother who had been ever kind and gentle. It was a practical world now, and imagination in its midst was out of place. Moreover, my pupilage at Welsdon had not been all lost time, and, thanks to the teaching of a man more shrewd in his particular knowledge than I had ever met, the farm gave promise of being a successful enterprise. I was happy in my own quiet, reserved way, that cared to make no sign. The time sped on with me; life seemed settling down; all the old past friends might have vanished for ever for the signs they gave of their existence, and the bygone time might be the fragment of a novel ending in uncertainty. Fourteen months, or thereabouts, since I had quitted the farm at Follingay; the harvest in, the wheat sold at a fair price per quarter, the farm-stock thriving, the evenings "drawing in," my mother and I companions by the fire we took to so early in the Vale of St. John. A quiet, homespun life in the valley; primitive times over again, with nothing to disturb the even tenor of my way; life monotonous, yet not unpleasant. With more friends round me, I might have reached to something higher than the quiet, reserved happiness to which I have alluded. And after all, was happiness such as mine more or less than resignation?

My mother and I were by the fireside:

my mother knitting complacently, and listening to the book that I was reading —the cat purring between us, and blessing in her heart the chilly evenings that had brought the fires round so early. And in the midst of this home picture came a friend from the times I was living down, and took his place between me and my mother, and laid his honest hand upon my shoulder, with a suddenness that made me start.

"William Grey!"

"I bribed the servants to spare me an announcement," said Grey, laughing at my amazement; "and here I am, like the ghost of my old self—coming to prove that I am in the habit of keeping my word. Mrs. Neider," turning to my mother, "I hope the name of William Grey of Welsdon is not quite foreign to you?"

"My dear son has often spoken of his fellow-pupils," replied my mother, rising and making her best curtsey, and offering him both her plump, mittened hands; "friends of my Alfred are the best friends of his mother."

"I need not doubt that, looking into the mother's face, and knowing what true mothers have been."

The tones of his voice struck me, and I regarded him more closely. I had not observed till then he was in mourning.

"You have had a loss?"

"Yes—a few months ago I lost my mother," said Grey. "Two months after her death my father married again—a neighbour's daughter, who, they say, is to present me in good time with a little half sister. That will make eighteen of us."

He laughed at the probable increase to his family; but it was not the same pleasant laugh with which he had favoured us a moment or two since.

"She's a very good sort," he added; "though she don't agree with my eldest sisters quite so well as my father expected. However, they jog along pretty well, and as my sisters are marrying, and my brothers setting up for themselves, she is becoming happier every day. My mother had money in her own right, and bequeathed it amongst us—my share has bought me a farm, Edmonton way. A nice farm enough, and within an easy distance of town, but horribly dull for a single young fellow like me."

He sat between us, and lifted the cat on his knees as an *amende honorable* for disturbing her; and puss took a fancy to him on the instant, and was evidently a judge of human nature.

"So, the harvest being in, Neider, I relieve the monotony of my position by a tour in the lake district; winding up with an ascent of Mount Skiddaw, and a descent into Keswick and the Vale of St. John, wherein peacefully nestles the farm of an old friend. And being here, and fond of com-

pany, I intend to stay till I grow trouble-
some."

"Stay till I tell you to go, Grey."

"Perhaps I will," said he, drily—" and
now to business."

I formed a pretty fair guess concerning
the nature of the business that had brought
him hither, although he turned to my
mother, and excluded me from a share in
the conversation.

"Mrs. Neider, I am a solitary young
man, with a large farm on my hands. My
brothers hate farming, and will have
nothing to do with me; my sisters are city
young ladies, and have husbands to look
after in town, and consider farming life low.
The farm properly managed is likely to be
good property, but it's rather a large one,
and more than one young fellow's work. I
require a partner to assist me with a little of
his capital and more of his common sense;
and if that partner's in the happy possession
of a mother who can undertake the domes-

ticities, I am so much nearer peace and quietness. Now, your little boy "—with a comical glance over his shoulder at me— " would suit me very well, and I should suit your little boy, because I should let him have his own way, and he's rather fond of it. That's how the matter stands—so shake hands, Mrs. Neider, and say it's all settled."

My mother sat with her eyes very much distended, and her breath entirely gone. William Grey's volubility was a little too much for her.

" M-m-my dear Alfred," she gasped forth at last—" what does Mr. Grey mean ? "

" Alfred, belay there ! " cried Grey, waving his hand behind him; " your turn for talk will come in good time. At present Mrs. Neider is on her legs—beg pardon," said he, reddening, "but it's a Parliamentary term, and implies that we wait your opinion on the case."

" But I don't understand you, Mr. Grey,"

said my mother; "if you will only allow my Alfred to speak — he's so very clear-sighted."

"All a mother's prejudice, and I don't believe a word of it," said Grey; "your experience of life, your seniority, entitle you to the first opinion. I have a farm too large for me, and require a partner. This farm can't be very profitable, must be horribly sloppy—and the sooner it is sold the better, take an honest man's word for it."

"But yours is a large farm, sir, and near London, where land is expensive, and——"

"Mother," I interrupted, "Mr. Grey has not fully considered this matter—he would be the victim of his own generous impulse. There is too much to consider to decide hastily on so important a question."

"I don't see it," said Grey—"'strike while the iron is hot' is my motto."

"And 'more haste is worse speed' is mine."

" Oh ! you have always something in that hard head to interfere with something in my—soft one—eh ? "

" Soft heart, Grey."

" Get out with you ! "

The subject was deferred for that night; but Grey was ready for the charge the following morning—spoke of his old idea, that it would happen thus some day, and denied indignantly that there was any impulse in the matter. It required considerable sifting to ascertain that his farm was a valuable one, and that an equal share in it was far beyond our humble means. Still he pressed me so hard to my own advantage—not alone a pecuniary one, but the advantage of a true friend's society—that the final resolution was to sell the farm in Cumberland, and buy with its proceeds a share, proportionate to the available capital, in William Grey's farm near Edmonton.

Before the Christmas came round, we had left the grand Cumberland scenery far behind us, and were domiciled for good in our new farm. And here life began again, and the old figures of the past came from the background into the light of every day.

# CHAPTER II.

## AN EVENING PARTY.

I HAD fairly settled down to my change in life when a letter, that had been addressed to my farm in Cumberland, followed me to my new address. Opening it I discovered a letter from Nicholas Thirsk:—

"Bedford Square,
"Feb. 16th, 1858.

"MY DEAR NEIDER,—Can an old friend induce you to travel a couple of hundred miles to celebrate so important an event as the coming of age of Mrs. Nicholas Thirsk on the 23rd instant? Important to her, me,

and the heir of the house of Thirsk, whose
vociferous remonstrance against a change of
linen wells to my ears in the study, wherein
I am locked, thinking how I can best greet a
faithful comrade, and induce him to shake
hands with me.  I am afraid a formal invitation might have deterred you—an indignant remonstrance at your forgetfulness
have given rise to a counter-charge—so I
write to the Cumberland farm, and say
simply, '*Come!*'  There isn't a friend in
the world whom I should be so glad to see.

"I hope you will believe that I remain,

"Ever faithfully yours,

"NICHOLAS THIRSK.

"A. Neider, Esq."


It was a hastily written letter, but it was
one that afforded me no small satisfaction.
It spoke of his friendship, and assured me that
in the midst of his new bright world I had
not been forgotten.  There was less sign of
the reckless dash of the past in his few hur-

ried words; he wrote in good spirits; but the mocking air, the crude sceptical comments on everything around him, were entirely absent. He even signed himself " ever faithfully " without a sneer at all believers in men's affections and gratitude. He wrote simply as one who remembered me with many kindly feelings; and reading the epistle, I could believe that his runaway match had not proved an unhappy one. He had married a wife who brought him riches with her one-and-twentieth year, and he had always spoken of wealth as a *summum bonum*, and scoffed at those who thought otherwise. True, it appeared at first sight that it was a love-match also; and love and money together must constitute as much perfect happiness as ordinary mortals can expect.

"What do you think of this?" I said, passing the letter to Grey.

"It reads well," said Grey, with some hardness in his tones. He had been always a little jealous of my interest in Thirsk. And yet a more unselfish, good-tempered fellow never existed.

"I fancy he must have altered for the better."

"Very probably — what do you mean to do?"

"Answer the letter."

"And accept the invitation to a grand party in Bedford Square?"

"Well—why not?"

"Oh! I can't say why not," said Grey; "unless aristocratic *réunions* should give you your old distaste for farming. Thirsk belongs to a sphere widely different from ours, and *must* naturally look down upon us."

"I shall not seek to intrude upon his sphere, Grey," I answered, "and I am very sensible of the difference between a farmer and a gentleman. Still, he presses me this once—and it is an especial case."

"And as your heart is set upon it, go by all means," said Grey, "but, my dear old fellow, don't come back with your head in the air because you've been asked to an evening party at a house in Bedford Square."

"Has it ever struck you that I was likely to be affected by a little more outward show than we indulge in at this farm, Grey?"

"Of course it hasn't, and I'm a jealous beast, who want my head punched. I know what is the true reason, though!"

"What?"

"It's because he hasn't asked me, and I can't swell about in a dress-coat—like one of the cock-sparrow tribe. I doubt if there are any white kid gloves made to fit my hands, they've begun to spread so beautifully!"

I was laughing at his remark, when he said very suddenly and quickly—

"You'll make every inquiry about old friends. I should be glad to hear that they are all happy, you know?"

I hardly understood him for the moment, when he said, more quickly still—

" Mercy Ricksworth, I mean. That old flame of mine," he added, with an abrupt, unnatural laugh.

" My dear fellow, you don't——"

" Don't think of her now, you mean," he said, with a heightened colour; " well, I don't more than I can help, because it's not good for me. But I told you long ago that I was one who never changed—and to hear she was happy and contented would be good news to me—that's all."

" I hope to bring you good news, then."

Grey changed the topic at once, and we were presently speaking of sowing and seeding, and other topics foreign to that little romantic past which Nicholas Thirsk's letter had helped to revive.

I answered this letter, accepting the writer's invitation for the twenty-third instant, adding a few less formal sentences that might help to prove my memory of the past days was not unfaithful, and winding up with intelligence that I had left Cumberland and was a partner with William Grey in a surburban farm. I had had an idea that he would have written a second invitation to Grey upon the receipt of this intelligence, but I was doomed to disappointment, and started on my journey to London alone.

A long journey in a hired fly from Edmonton to the west-end of town— ensconced in a corner of the vehicle in all the glory of full dress. My admiring mother affirmed that I had never looked so nice, and Grey recommended me to search for a second heiress, as heiresses appeared to conduce to a happy frame of mind.

I do not know that I felt particularly nervous at the prospect that lay before me— that I thought there was anything to seriously disturb me at my first entrance into the dazzling arena of fashionable life. I had been brought up quietly, seen little company, knew not much of London; but, still, I did not experience any nervous trepidation at the thought of meeting Nicholas Thirsk in a society concerning which I knew nothing. I had confidence in my own knowledge of the common civilities and formalities to be used on such occasions, and I was not naturally of a bashful disposition. I felt I should be out of my element, but that I should attract any particular degree of attention to that fact, I did not anticipate. I could dance, I could talk to a certain extent; I had a bass voice, or three notes towards one—I had attended a few parties in Germany, where my father, in his love for the " Vaterland," had insisted upon my completing my education—and Nicholas Thirsk, gentleman, should not have cause to be ashamed of that friend whom he had honoured by his invitation.

I arrived in London at a somewhat late hour. The proprietor of the livery stables at Edmonton had not favoured me with a very agile steed, and the clocks were striking ten when I shook off the cramp in my legs, and leaped from the carriage to the pavement, over which an awning had been erected from the kerbstone to the front door. Visitors were arriving every instant, and that part of the square was lively with the voices of the unwashed, who crowded to catch glimpses of the guests, and were kept in rank by two members of the metropolitan police-force.

I was making for the steps, when a voice amidst one half of the crowd on my left exclaimed very rapidly, " Mr. Neider !" and, turning at the moment, I fancied that there was a face amongst the mob of faces that was singularly familiar to me. Still, I was puzzled, and went up the steps and into the hall, before it struck me that it was Sir Richard Freemantle whom I had recognized ; then I hesitated whether to return and speak with him or not.

I resolved upon not returning. Sir Richard appeared merely to have mentioned my name aloud in his surprise at seeing me.

When I had looked in his direction, his features had assumed their characteristic immobility, and he had not uttered a second word to denote a desire to detain me. It appeared strange that the only brother of her whose majority so many were about to celebrate, was outside there amongst an inquisitive mob, possibly an uninvited guest. It spoke of the old feud still existent; of the baronet's pride, or Nicholas Thirsk's resentment, still keeping apart brother and sister. Remembering the conversation between me and Sir Richard, in the early times before the shock of the elopement had been received—of the wish that he had expressed to forgive all, and take his place by the side of one he loved—was to present before me a dark picture of the fierce enmity which Thirsk could nourish against his seeming foes, even when his plans had baffled them, and left them desolate.

"Mr. Alfred Neider!"

Some one had taken my hat; a second had asked my name and bawled it up the staircase; a third had opened a door and shouted it into a large, brilliantly-lighted room, whence music sounded, and where guests were dancing.

An instant afterwards, and Nicholas Thirsk, in evening dress, was before me.

"My dear Neider, how glad I am to see you!"

He shook my hand in his, his dark eyes danced again with pleasure at meeting me—there was no doubt I was a welcome guest.

"Why, how you've altered, Neider!"

"Seventeen months make a difference. I see a great change in my co-pupil."

"Say for the better, man."

"For the better—if it had been for the worse, I should have kept my opinion to myself."

"So should I, perhaps," he added; "well, why don't you flatter me? Don't I look as if the new life agreed with me, and as if this were the sphere I was born to flutter my wings in?"

"It seems to agree with you."

"Just as short as ever, Alf Neider—as if I could stand your German uncouthness, now I am a great man!"

"You will not mind it for one evening, Thirsk?"

"Do you mean that you vanish away like a ghost down a trap after this festal night?"

"We belong to two worlds—a wanderer from mine would be an intruder on yours."

"I'll argue that point with you another time. I wandered from a sphere similar to this to a lower, and I was unhappy, discontented, 'anything by turns.' But I could have started from a low estate to this with singular complacency. Neider, old boy, I think I have a berth under Government to offer you. I was talking to a big, bouncing secretary yesterday."

"Thank you—but I am fixed to farming for life."

"Truly bucolic! Did you ever read Gesner?"

"Yes."

"Ah! he has infected you with pastoral notions," said he, his old satiric spirit peering out for the first time; "he stands in the way of the advancement I offer you. Is it he, or a more modern, less high-minded being, yclept William Grey?"

"William Grey, I am inclined to fancy," I said; "but surely you haven't asked me here to satirize me and my friends?"

"Right, Neider—and shame to the host who would attempt it, and a good kicking at the same time, if you can get to his side of the mahogany. This way, Mrs. Thirsk is anxious to see you."

"You flatter me."

"On my honour, no."

He passed his arm through mine, and led me down the room. The music had ceased by this time, the dance was over, and the guests were promenading, gossiping, talking scandal, and making love.

A brilliant crowd, through which we threaded our way—if not particularly aristocratic, and boasting in its midst few titles, still a fair sample of the upper English society. And Thirsk moved therein with easy grace; he was right, I thought, it was his natural sphere, and in returning to it he had left behind much of that false misanthropy which had been the attribute of the past wherein I had known him, and misjudged him.

There was a little knot of people near the raised orchestra at the end of the room—a few gentlemen and ladies, amongst whom I had no difficulty in recognizing the Agatha Freemantle of old times.

She was looking pale, I fancied, and the white dress she wore appeared to be ill-chosen for a complexion never very roseate.

She looked a girl still; her slight figure and

her childish face scarcely warranted one in
believing that this was the heroine of the
night. Looking so young and delicate a wife
and mother, she awakened more interest in
herself than admiration at her charms.
She had never been a pretty girl, notwith-
standing that her features were more regular
than one-half of the ladies there who laid a
claim to beauty. It was not a want of
animation either, or a deficiency of grace,
which suggested that she was far from a
pretty woman; and yet I could not have
said what conveyed the impression to me—
what had even suggested it before then in
the hasty glimpses I had had of her.

Still that night she awakened no common
interest; the world had heard of her marriage for love, and the out-of-way means by
which it had been effected. The world,
always adding more shadows to a story
than there is any occasion for, had made a
romance of this one; Sir Richard Freemantle was the grim guardian and the evil

genius—an anchorite and an ascetic, with a heart as hard as the stones he had made a study of—a man who had sought to quench all light and life from his half-sister's path, and set an interdict on love-making. And Agatha Freemantle had been endowed with all the virtues—she had a great many—and the world, which had not had a runaway match to gloat over for many a month, applauded the unwise step, and thought how happily it all had ended. Virtue and true love rewarded at the altar, and the evil genius, the flinty-hearted baronet, sinking down a trap into the caves of gloom and despair.

Exactly how all the novels and plays ended, and as true to life as most of them !

"Agatha — here is our old friend Mr. Neider at last."

"I am glad to see he has not disappointed us," said she; her gloved hand rested in my own, and she welcomed me as though I had been an old friend of hers as well as her husband's. The little knot of fashionables melted imperceptibly away; and Nicholas Thirsk, saying, "Take care of Mrs. Thirsk," left me to pay my small civilities to the hostess.

There was only one topic on which I could discourse, or in which I could expect to interest her—her husband. I was well assured that she could grow eloquent on that theme, and that it would relieve the mutual embarrassments we felt.

Having congratulated her on attaining her majority, and wishing her the usual compliments, for which she thanked me, I alluded at once to Nicholas Thirsk. We were seated side by side then, near the orchestra.

"I am pleased to see so great an alteration in him."

"Do you think he has altered much?"

"Yes."

"And for the better?"

"Certainly."

"Sometimes I think so myself, and yet sometimes—" she paused, and then made a dart back to the old subject, "and he thinks so too. He is more at home of course than at Follingay Farm—but they were," with a little sigh that did not escape me, "very happy times for me."

"All has ended as happily as a pleasant story-book," I said.

"Yes—we are both very happy. Oh! there is nothing in the way of our felicity —he said there never should be. Do you think this a happy scene, now, Mr. Neider?"

"Judging by the surface of things, how can I doubt it?"

"Oh! I like my quiet evenings best," she cried, with a girlish enthusiasm that was very winning and natural; "I am always very happy when Nicholas is at home with me and baby—Nicholas relating his adventures at the Farm, or else reading to me—I like his own writings best."

" Does he write much ?"

"Very seldom," said his wife, with another little sigh; "and he can write so well, if he likes. He don't see the occasion, he says; and I believe sometimes the chance of being famous is slipping through his hands."

" I must talk to him," said I, half-jestingly.

" If you only would!" she cried, with an impulsive earnestness that startled me; " I am sure he thinks so much of you, and all you say. He has told me twenty times how highly he holds you in his estimation, and you might have more weight with him than I."

" I am sure you over-estimate my power."

" If you would come some quiet evening, and coax him into the reading of a MS., now."

" I am so much his friend and confidant, that he has never confessed to me his literary abilities, Mrs. Thirsk."

" Indeed! And I have betrayed his con-

fidence—how cross he will be, to be sure!"
and she turned a shade paler at the thought.

"But I have heard that he possessed
some talent for authorship, through a friend
of his."

"Mr. Genny?"

"Yes."

"He will be here to night."

"And Mrs. Genny?" I asked, eagerly.

"Yes—I think so. Heigho! a light-
hearted, loving woman, with a cheering
word for all—I wish I had her spirits."

This was a new subject to ponder over,
as the music rang out again, and the dancers flitted by. A light-hearted woman!—
she who had been so grave and thoughtful,
and hated frivolity. Everything around
me was on the change, and only I retained
my old austerity. Words that Harriet had
said to me in the latter days, before the
wedding ring was on her finger, came with
full force upon me: "If we should ever
meet again, you will find me in a new cha-

racter—the true character, which I have hidden here." Did I treasure her every word so much, that, in the midst of all the gaiety around me, they recurred to me as forcibly as though they had been spoken in my ears that minute?

" You dance, Mr. Neider?"

" I have a misty reminiscence of some saltatory performances," I replied; "but I —I hope I am not keeping you from any participation in the general festivity."

" Oh! no—I have had enough dancing for this evening—but I was afraid of wearying you with my egotistical prattle, as Nicholas calls it."

"And I fear I am monopolizing too much of the hostess's attention," I said; " and clashing against all rules of etiquette."

" Are you in favour of a strict observance of those rules, Mr. Neider?"

" Well, I can't say I am."

She dropped her fan into her lap, to clap her gloved hands with delight at my reply.

"I'll tell Nicholas that—I am so glad his Orestes or Damon whom he quotes so often, agrees with me in that. Would you believe that I make him quite cross at times, by what he terms my frightful impulsiveness?"

"His cross fits were very evanescent, in my time."

"Oh! he can be very firm and angry sometimes, like the rest of your sex," she said, "and make no allowance for the impulse that carries me a little way from the beaten track. He forgets it made a happy wife of me."

"And a happy husband of him, I am sure."

"Ye-es."

She was trifling with her bouquet now, and the white leaves of an exotic were dropping round her dress. She looked up, caught my observant glance, and turned her head hastily away. Did she fear there was something in her face that might betray her?

"Do you see that old gentleman entering the card-room?" she asked, suddenly.

"The short old gentleman who stoops so much?"

"The same."

"That is Sir Nicholas Thirsk, my husband's father."

"I am very glad to see him here," I ejaculated; "it is a witness of a better understanding between the father and the son."

"Yes; they are friends again. It was strange that the step which parted me from a brother I loved, should have reconciled· Nicholas to a father who had been hard and unjust to him for many years. And if Richard were a little hard upon me now and then, he was never unjust."

Here was a chance to say a good word for Sir Richard Freemantle, and I had promised the worthy baronet to say it on the first opportunity that presented itself. If I could dispel a little of the mist, and bring brother and sister to a better understanding of each other, I should have done no small good in accepting Thirsk's invitation.

" I hoped to have seen Sir Richard here?"

" My brother here!" she cried, amazed; "whatever made you think Sir Richard Freemantle would be here? He objects to society."

" But he loves his sister, and she attains to-day an age which he must have often thought of and looked forward to."

" He would not have come if he had been asked," she said, speaking with great rapidity; "and I dare not ask him; Nicholas does not admire him much, and thinks a reconciliation between us would bring about much recrimination, quarrelling, everything but the good-will that might naturally be expected. I don't know—I think Nicholas must be right, although he speaks at times so bitterly of Richard."

"Forbidden ground, Mr. Neider!" said a sharp voice by our side, and the subject of our conversation stood looking at his wife with a less amiable expression of countenance than he had hitherto worn that evening, so far as my experience went.

"Forgive me, Nicholas dear; Mr. Neider passes so rapidly from one subject to another —and, in fact, Mr. Neider is to blame for mentioning the subject."

And she appeared rather relieved and delighted at having shifted the onus of responsibility on to my shoulders.

"What, have we a traitor in the camp?" he said, turning to me with the frown no longer on his brow.

"I hope not."

"You are ignorant of the rules governing us and our household gods," said he, lightly. "I think I must write somewhere about these rooms: 'No mention of Sir Richard Freemantle here, except on business of importance.' Neider, you are wasting too much time.

I've been asked by half-a-dozen young
ladies, who is the interesting young man
with the bumps on his forehead, and the
whiskers too big for him. You must dance,
man, and be lively and do honour to the
feast. This is a day to be marked with a
white stone!"

He shook me by the shoulder in his
excitement. On the threshold of wealth
and independence, he could afford to be a
little extravagant.

"Come with me, and let me introduce
you to a young lady with two thousand
a-year. There's a wen under one ear, but
it's only a little one."

"Nicholas!" said his wife, reproachfully.

"And that may be gilded to look handsome, *mon brave*," he cried. "Agatha,"
turning to her, "bustle about, my girl, and
don't mope any more in a corner, as if all
the troubles in life had arrived with your
coming of age. Neider, do you dance?"

"I believe so. It's so long ——"

" Here, practice the next quadrille with Mrs. Thirsk. You're too nervous to distinguish yourself before the young lady I spoke of, at present. I shall be on the watch, and pounce down on you like a Wehrwolf of your own native land."

" That's England."

" Oh! your confounded German name always makes me think you of foreign ex traction. Will you have any wine? "

" Not now, thank you."

" Run through a quadrille, then—I shall be your *vis-à-vis*, if I can manage it, if only for the sake of throwing you into a muddle."

He did manage it, but he failed in his object, even if he had ever intended it, of throwing me into confusion. I had a good memory, and Mrs. Thirsk and I being a side couple, I could take stock of our predecessor's manœuvres, and save covering myself with ignominy. The quadrille finished, Thirsk having conducted his partner to a seat by his wife, put his arm through mine and hurried me away.

"What's the next movement, Thirsk?"

"'Should auld acquaintance be forgot,'" sang he; "this way, Farmer Neider, for just a glimpse at another little world, where the head has more to do than the heels."

He drew me into the card-room, where a dozen people or more were playing whist and loo. The whist party sat in a remote corner, with a table-lamp to themselves, and one of the four was Sir Nicholas Thirsk?

"Watch that ancient gentleman," said Nicholas, pointing towards him.

"Well."

"If he were playing whist for his soul, he could not be more eager," remarked his son; "and his soul *is* in the hope of winning the five shilling stakes. You very seldom find a lover of fossils and bits of rocks such a *gourmand* at crown pieces. Now, guess who that gentleman is?"

"Sir Nicholas Thirsk."

"Confound it! did Agatha tell you that?"

" Yes."

" Upon my soul, she has given you a fair sketch of everything and everybody in a little time. Did you ever meet with a girl who talked so much in your life?"

" She appears an artless, affectionate woman—you should consider yourself a lucky man."

" So I am. Don't I go down to the Tramlingford Bank to-morrow, to draw therefrom, as her husband, the sum of sixty thousand pounds?"

" I mean lucky in your wife, not in her money, Thirsk."

" She finds little fault with me," he said, laughing; "and she thinks me a paragon and a wonderful clever being, blessed with three-fourths of the virtues under the sun, and only a quarter of the most respectable vices. By George! she's right in one thing."

" What is that?"

" You do slip away, like an eel, from one subject to another—only a moment since I was speaking of my father."

" And you led me away from the topic by a right-angled question."

" As we were, then. You perceive my father and I are friends?"

" Yes."

" He's a cunning old gentleman himself, and the bold stroke I made for a wife hit his fancy, and brought him and his blessing together.    He was kind enough to tell me that he always thought me too much of a fool ever to succeed in the world.    Shall I introduce you ?"

I drew back.

" Only my fun," said Thirsk; " he'd curse me till my dying day if I distracted him from his attention on the odd trick ; some other time, when the atmosphere is less charged with parental lightning.    Presto—who sits at the loo-table yonder?"

He gave a twirl to my arm, that nearly

wrenched it from the socket, and brought me face to face with Robin Genny. He was sitting on the opposite side of the table, and had he looked up at that moment would have recognized me. There was the game-ster's look upon his face; I fancied it was more haggard and lined with hard study than when I had seen it last, unless it was the excitement of the moment that seemed to have aged it wondrously quick. There was gold on the table, and the pursuit of gold will age a man more speedily than he bar-gains for.

"This is the devil's own table for sinners of magnitude — they play unlimited loo here."

"Is it a favourite game of Robin Genny's?"

"I cannot say that it is, particularly— some one has asked him to join, I suppose. Robin Genny is a jolly good fellow, who always does what he's asked. You look grave?"

"Indeed," said I, with a start; "I was not

aware of it. Do you think Robin Genny would come away if *you* asked him?"

" Very likely; it was for that experiment I brought you into this unholy temple. He's a poor devil, who can't afford to be looed seven or eight pounds at a time—clever man as he thinks himself. By the god of thieves, he has won the pool!"

There was excitement at the table; a flutter of rage, envy, and uncharitableness; Robin Genny, not pale and haggard now, but radiant as a peony. Sir Nicholas was heard to mutter something about "a damned uproar" over his cards.

"Genny," said Thirsk, sharply.

He looked up, smiled, and, with a half wrench of himself from the chair, came towards us.

"Fortune favours the bold card-player," said Thirsk; "here, profligate, behold our young and worthy farmer."

He shook me heartily by the hand.

"This is a meeting of old friends, relations, and acquaintances," said he. "I hope the world has been dealing fairly with you?"

"I can't complain," replied I. "May I expect the same answer from Mr. Genny?"

"I don't see why you should not," he said, "being in luck's way to-night. Blessed be the man who invented unlimited loo! Have you seen Harriet?"

"Not yet. I am anxious to pay my respects to her."

"Take care, Genny, this is an old rival."

"I can trust him," said Genny, shaking hands again; "and now, Thirsk, if you'll just ——"

"If you'll just do the polite yourself, and not set me trotting about the room in search of your amiable helpmate, you'll be performing a more graceful act than your woolly brains contemplate just at this minute."

"You always were an impertinent young beggar," said Genny laughing. "This way, Mr. Neider; let us leave the scoffer to himself."

We passed into the ball-room, into the whirl of dancers, flirters, and gossips ; where no shadows seemed to lurk, and where every serious thought was out of place amidst the dazzle of lights and harmony of music.

" He's doing it up grand," said Genny to me.

" He's what ? "

" Coming out—Thirsk of ours."

" Ah ! I understand."

" A lucky fellow in his way, but horribly extravagant," commented Genny ; " never a thought for the morrow—a black lily of the field, neither toiling nor spinning."

His criticism on Thirsk reminded me of Thirsk's comments on him — both verdicts might verge upon the truth.

"*Halte là !*" cried he to me suddenly. " Harriet, a ghost from Follingay Farm ! "

She was sitting very thoughtfully in one of the recesses of the window—the heavy folds of its drapery half hiding her from the gay crowd. She did not appear light-hearted then, I thought—it was the face of the farmer's niece I looked at anxiously.

She was standing before me smiling the instant afterwards—the first and the true love!

# CHAPTER III.

## MRS. GENNY.

She had not altered much, I thought. It was the clear frank face of the handsome woman I had ever known. It had always been — if I may term it so—an *unflinching* face; but it struck me as more apparent in that moment when a crowd of simperers and inanities were sweeping by. Yet there was nothing masculine in her face; it expressed woman's gentleness, forethought, sympathy, as much as it assured me that it was the countenance of one who would not give up at the first trouble, and cry *miserere!*

"I scarcely anticipated meeting so old a

friend at Mrs. Thirsk's ball," said she, shaking hands with me.

"Mr. Thirsk did not forget his brother-in-arms."

"I should not have thought you would have cared for a party of this description, Mr. Neider."

"Did she show any *penchant* for parties herself at Follingay Farm?" interrupted Genny, with a laugh.

"Oh! it was a world where our true characters took time to develop," said she; and then turning to me, "have you been dancing?"

"I have made one little attempt!"

"You are a most accomplished farmer!" she said, with a flash of her old brusqueness. "I should think your farm is likely to become a prosperous undertaking," she added, in a lighter tone, "if you leave it two hundred miles behind, and seek such réunions as these."

"This is my first appearance here, and

this, you must remember, is an exceptional night."

"For Mrs. Thirsk and her friends," she added, drily, "from whom I hope I am not detaining you?"

"Oh, no!" I answered; "I am a straw on the sea of fashionable life, and glad to seek shelter by the side of a friend. Am I keeping you from dancing?"

"My dancing days are over, Mr. Neider," said she, looking up with a laughing face towards her husband.

"I can persuade Harriet to attend these sorts of soirées now and then, Neider," he said, "but I can't make her do anything but sit and satirize the company,—like the crabbed old dowagers and the soured spinsters who sit with their bony backs against the walls of every ball-room."

"It is a new exemplification of the proverb concerning leading the mule to the water," said Mrs. Genny. "Robin, dear, what are you swaying from one foot to the other about, and looking so miserable?"

"Miserable!—that's a good one!"

"Have you been playing cards this evening?"

"Ye-es—a little."

"Well, you only promised to play a little; will you not sit down and keep Mr. Neider and me company?"

"Well, you see, I—I have left my cards on the table."

"Some one will soon take your place. What game were you playing?"

"Loo."

"For high stakes, of course?"

"Oh, no!—a few halfpence. I think I'll just finish my hand, Harriet."

"Very well, dear. You will remember that I don't wish to stay here too long?"

"I shall be back in a very few minutes."

"And if the gamblers become too excited, you'll think—oh! you'll think of the new dress you promised me last week!"

He laughed very heartily—even looked very affectionately towards her.

"You shall have twenty per cent. on the profits of the evening, my dear," said he, and hurried away.

I saw her look after him with a face that had lost all its smiles, till he disappeared between the curtains of the card-room.

"Loo was not a very expensive game, as we played it in the winter nights at Follingay Farm, Mr. Neider?" said she, turning to me.

"No."

"These great friends of my Robin indulge in heavier stakes, I suppose?" she said, with a carelessness that implied—almost too suspiciously—no particular interest in my answer.

"They may be rather more extravagant."

Robin Genny had gone, and there was no bringing him back. I could see no occasion to alarm his wife on the subject.

"Then Robin will be extravagant too;

he is an excellent copyist," said she, with a laugh that was new to me, for it was a forced laugh, and she had been above disguise in the times that were gone. "Farewell the flounced silk with which I sought to dazzle my neighbours!"

I laughed, too, at her remark. What a pair of hypocrites we were!

"Now, Mr. Neider, if you do not object to my distracting your attention from these waltzers, I should like to monopolize five minutes of your time."

I took the vacant seat beside her, and whilst the music sounded, and the waltzers spun past, and all the giddy, fashionable world seemed verging on delirium, we spoke of farming life, like a couple of prosaic country folk.

"Your farm in Cumberland—you have decided on keeping it?"

"I have sold it."

"Sold it!" she cried; "and given up farming life, after all your past assertions!"

" I have sold it, and invested my capital in a certain share of a farm belonging to William Grey."

" Grey and you are partners?"

" Yes."

"I am glad of that!" said she; "you could not have chosen a more sensible, practical, hard-working friend to offer you an example of honest perseverance."

" You speak as if I were a poor, vacillating mortal, Mrs. Genny."

"I meet you in a sphere above your own—I find you still the friend of a man who, whatever his virtues may be, has failings which are soon copied, and lead surely and swiftly to habits that must sap all principle. You may consider yourself a very firm-minded man, sir, but the force of evil example will prove too strong for you."

"I have confidence in my powers of self-command, even were I the bosom friend of the gentleman whom you mistrust so much."

" I say he has failings," said Mrs. Genny
—" that he is extravagant, and thoughtless,
is led farther than he thinks, and leads
others. Every story that I hear con-
firms me in my verdict."

" You speak severely."

" I may have cause," she said—then corrected herself hastily, " or I may soon have
cause, if my voice be powerless to persuade
my husband to give up so expensive an
acquaintance. A poor author, no more than
a young farmer, can afford the luxury of a
gentleman friend; one is likely to become .
envious of his good fortune, and tired of
one's efforts to earn in a week what the
evil example flings away in an hour.
You will excuse me speaking like a friend
to you ? "

" Excuse you, Mrs. Genny ? " I said—" I
thank you for your interest—I shall think
of your advice."

" You are a young man, and easily influenced."

"I am vain enough to think that you have made a mistake there," I replied.

She was thinking of the old days, when my heart was moved so deeply as to avow a love for her; from my actions in those days did she judge me ever a child, that a word might turn? It seemed so, and it irritated me. More, it assured me that she might judge falsely and hastily of others as well as myself, and take her views of life from misrepresented facts. She spoke bitterly of him beneath whose roof she sat there an invited guest—by whose example she feared her husband might be influenced.

"I daresay you wonder why I am here, Mr. Neider," she said, almost reading a portion of my thoughts.

"You appear to evince no particular affection for Mr. and Mrs. Thirsk."

"What do I know of them?"

"I—I thought Mr. Thirsk was a friend of Mr. Genny's."

" But not of mine. I have seen him but twice since my marriage—why should I evince any affection towards him ? If pity be akin to love, I may soon clasp his childish wife to my heart."

" She is very happy, she assures me."

Mrs. Genny gave a toss to her head—she would hear nothing in defence. For a woman ever light-hearted, she was certainly out of temper that evening. And for a man who loved good temper in his friends, it was strange—it had been ever strange— what a wondrous charm her fretful moods had always had for me.

" Evincing no affection " (the words seemed to have aggravated her, she re-iterated them so frequently), " you must wonder why I am here. Perhaps because it would have been very dull at home sitting up for Mr. Genny—perhaps because I take this opportunity of seeing an infatuated girl."

" Infatuated ? "

" Yes — Mercy Ricksworth, infatuated with her mistress's merits—ready to die for her if it were necessary—and sounding ever her wondrous praises in my ears; as if a woman cared to hear the praises of another —as if it were the nature of our sex !"

She was becoming more angry every instant.

"What a jealous, cross woman I am growing !" she cried, impatiently, " to let a stranger like you see that I am envious of Mercy's love for her mistress, and think it should have been mine by a natural right. The mistress loves and trusts in her—and Mercy is a girl to love and be loved ; as impulsive as her mistress, and with almost as strange a view of life and life's duties. Yes, I am a very jealous woman, and, for one whose own path is so clear of briars and pitfalls,"—(did she speak then with a curling lip ?—I fancied so)—" for one whose husband has never given her a single harsh word during sixteen months of wedlock, it is a little remarkable. If Robin would only scold me, and be more firm with me, and read me lectures on the spirit of unchari-tableness with which I am possessed !"

She shook off her ill mood like a water-drop, and talked of the ball, and the dancer's dresses, and the dancers themselves —and uttered many remarks on passing things, with a pleasant *naïveté* that told me what an agreeable companion, what a cheerful wife she was to Robin Genny.

And while I was thinking of that, she said suddenly—

" Where's this card-room ?—are there any ladies there ?"

" Do you think the love of gain, or of coveting our neighbour's goods, is only con-fined to the masculine gender ?"

" Perhaps not more than three-fourths of those weaknesses," she said, caustically ; " will you lend me your arm to the card-room ?"

" You have really made up your mind
not to dance this evening ?"

" I am not fond of dancing."

I offered her my arm, and we went
together towards the card-room, at the door
of which she turned angrily away.

" No—he mustn't think his wife can't
trust him!" she cried; then glanced nervously
towards me, to see if I had caught her words
—which I had, though I feigned to be
intensely interested in steering my way
through the guests.

" On second thoughts, I think I will take
this opportunity of wishing Mrs. Thirsk
many happy returns of the day," said she;
" we passed her a few minutes since."

We turned and found Mrs. Thirsk gossiping pleasantly with some ladies;
Harriet Genny drew her hand from my
arm.

" Shall I see you again, to bid you good
night ?" she inquired.

" I think so."

"If not—good night to you. I am glad to have met an old friend, and to have found him well in health, strong of will, and a man of the world."

"And I am glad to have found you well and happy, if a little distrustful of my future steps."

"I am not distrustful," she replied; "you will work your way in the world, I hope. Do you take offence at a friendly warning —*you*?"

"God forbid!"

"Good night, then."

We shook hands and parted. I went immediately to the card-room.

She was Robin Genny's wife, and beyond all hope of mine; but her thoughts I fancied I could read, and they would trouble mine, and set me sharing them. She was fearful of her husband's strength of mind, although her woman's pride fought hard not to betray that fear to me, and lower him she had married in my eyes. If I could, after my own fashion, lure Robin Genny from the spell that kept him to the card-room.

He was playing unlimited loo still. There were six players at the table, five of them young men, one old and grey-haired. There was a little crowd of watchers of the game; dancers, who had strolled in with their partners for a moment, and had become interested in the hard fight for the glistening heap of gold and silver in the centre of the table. The players were all pale and excited, with a strange fire in their eyes; it had become a something more than play. In matters of life and death I had seen men less serious; amongst actors in a barn, I had seen better attempts to appear easy in mind, and laugh now and then in a natural manner. Robin Genny was not winning then. It was a scene that I was glad a wife's pride had spared the farmer's niece.

I went behind him and laid my hand

suddenly on his shoulder. Had it been the touch of a bailiff, he could not have jumped more.

" Ah, Neider—what is it ?"

" If you have had enough of contesting Fortune's chances," said I, "come and drink a glass of wine with me. I am all alone in a world a trifle too civilized, and it's dull work."

He glanced at me irresolutely. He was one that might be led, I had been told more than once, and I was attempting the experiment. The players frowned at me as he sat with the pack of cards in his hands waiting to deal.

" I'll be with you in a moment, Neider. Where's Thirsk ? "

" I don't know—I have lost him," I replied; " we must look him up together —come on."

" I think I'll have my deal. Confound it, I have paid for that and my loo too, and have a right to a splash."

There was a general laugh as he commenced dealing. I heard one gentleman behind me whisper to a fair partner at his side—

" Genny the author."

" Genny—Genny," said the girl, trying
hard to remember the name.

" He's a magazine writer and an essayist
—one of the hard, dry species, whose genius
you ladies do not properly appreciate. One
of the soundest and clearest reasoners we
have."

"He seems very fond of cards," she
whispered.

It was a satire on clear reasoning, on practice and precept, that amused them both, and
they turned away laughing very heartily.
Meanwhile Genny had dealt, found nothing
in his hand, thrown it aside, and was
watching the progress of the game amongst
those who had been blessed with better
cards than he.

I touched him on the shoulder again.

" Now Genny ! "

He rose and left the table.

" Are you coming back again? " asked his neighbour.

" N—no, I think not. Haven't I had enough of it?"

There was another hearty laugh, especially from those who had won. They almost split their sides laughing.

" The shorn sheep retires to think of the lost wool that would have made him so comfortable this cold weather. *Au revoir*, gentlemen!"

He bore his losses well—he went away laughing with the rest. He liked to see the world smiling at his jests.

" Have you been unlucky, Genny ? "

" A little," he said, carelessly ; " nothing to go into deep mourning for. Let us have the wine—where did you leave Harriet? "

" Talking with Mrs. Thirsk."

" I hope she's making herself comfortable —she does not take kindly to evening parties and society in general. And the result of it is, she would make a hermit of me."

"But the hermitage might be as pleasant as here."

"She is a merry-hearted, busy, witty little helpmate," said Genny with enthusiasm, "but one can't be at home always, however much she may brighten it; and being a scribe, one must spend half his life with the Lares. Why, here is Harriet!"

Harriet, with her opera cloak drawn tightly round her as though she were cold, met us face to face.

"Were you coming for me?" he asked.

"For you?—no," she answered; "don't you think you can be trusted by yourself?"

He laughed at her light remark; he had forgotten the anxious look with which we had met her.

"Neider and I are going to have a glass of wine together—the reprobate comes like fate between me and my luck, and bears me away."

" Or like a guardian angel between you and desperation," said she, still laughing. But the lips only smiled—and what thoughtful eyes they were !

" Oh ! he's too stout for an angel !" cried Genny ; " what a jolly profession farming must be, to make all you fellows so wide. Why, I can see through my hand !"

And as he held it towards the light, I noticed how thin and almost transparent it was. At this moment a servant in livery touched me on the arm.

" You are Mr. Neider, I am told, sir ? "

" Yes."

" I am desired to give you this note," he said, with a reverential salaam, after tucking the salver under his arm.

I opened the letter, stared at the contents, looked at Mr. and Mrs. Genny.

" Not bad news, I hope ? " said the author's wife.

" Not that I am aware of—I hope not. Will you excuse me ? "

"We are going away soon. I do not think we shall wait for supper," said Harriet. "Shall we, dear?" turning to her husband.

"Well, just as you like."

"There are all the proof sheets at home; such a large pile, Robin."

"Ah! yes—I don't think we shall wait supper, Neider."

So I bade them good night, and I fancied that Harriet Genny parted rather coldly with me—too much like the acquaintance of an hour. Did she resent my interference, or was she vexed that she had betrayed to me a desire to lure her husband from the card-table? One or the other, I fancied, gave a distance to her speech and mien.

Outside the ball-room, and hesitating on the staircase, where the servants lounged, I met with a hindrance to my further progress. Nicholas Thirsk came up the stairs, three steps at a time, in his haste to rejoin his friends.

" Well, Neider, what's up ? " he cried familiarly.

" I am going away for a little while. I have an appointment which I feel compelled to keep."

" Strange!" said he, looking at me with a suspicion that I could not account for; " shall you be long ? "

" I think not."

" We sup at one o'clock. There will be a little speech-making I expect, and the health of Mrs. Thirsk drunk with all the honours. You will not fail me ? "

We drew out watches and compared the time. It was twenty minutes past eleven.

" I can promise, at least, to drink Mrs. Thirsk's health at supper."

" Thank you. I say !" he called, when I had made two or three steps down the stairs.

" What is it ? "

" I shall put down the young lady with

the wen for your especial escort into the supper-room."

And his laughing face looked over at me as I descended the stairs, laughing too. It was the last bright look on it for many a long day!

# CHAPTER IV.

## BAD NEWS.

THE missive that had so suddenly hurried me from the house of Nicholas Thirsk contained but a few lines. It was headed "*Private*," and ran thus:—

"DEAR SIR,

"May I beg to see you for a few moments? Business of *great importance* to me, and of still more importance to your friends, compels me to adopt this strange course. I shall be waiting for you at the corner of the first street to the left.

"Yours, in haste,

"RICHARD FREEMANTLE."

Had it been written by one who was a stranger to me, I should have probably declined the mysterious meeting; but that Sir Richard Freemantle desired an interview with me without a reasonable motive for so doing, was not, at first sight, probable. I did not anticipate a revelation of any "great importance," albeit Sir Richard had underlined the words; but I could not in common courtesy dissent to an interview with the baronet, though he might have nothing more to deliver to me than a message of love and congratulations to his sister, from whose home her husband's interdict debarred him.

I had some difficulty in finding the custodian of the hats and coats, in whom I recognized Mr. Ipps, formerly of Follingay Farm. He was sitting in a small room near the entry, with his feet on the fender, and his knees almost between the bars. I think he must have been dozing, for, as I entered the room with the servant who was

my escort, he started, and kicked the fire-
irons noisily about the fender.

"Now, old clumsy!" said the footman.

"Now, young jackanapes!" returned he,
with that old readiness at retcrt which I had
noted on my first meeting with him.

"This gentleman wants his hat and coat
—and you're asleep, as usual."

"Ax the gentleman's pardon."

There were but a few greatcoats in the room
—the majority of guests having come from a
short distance, and in their carriages. As I
had intended to stay in London that night, and
possibly the greater portion of the next day,
my careful mother had not only pressed my
over-coat upon me, but a whole portmanteau of luggage, which I had found, too late
for restitution, at the bottom of the fly. I
had no difficulty in finding my coat and
hat, and was retiring with that portion of
my wearing apparel, when Ipps touched me
timidly on the arm.

"I'm not intruding, Measter Neider?"

said he, wistfully—"I'm not too bould?"

" No—Ipps—what is it?"

"I should loike to know how the old measter is?"

"Very well, I believe.   I have not heard from him lately."

"You may tell him, I made a blessed mess of cooming here—an ould dissatisfied deevil that I wor!"

"What good can I do by telling him that?"

"Oh! he'll laugh a little, because he said Lunnon ways wouldn't suit an old man of eighty-four.   And he's so maun pleased when his word cooms true."

"I think you would have been better in the country, if——"

"If I could have kep' honest," he concluded, finishing my speech for me; "roight you be, sir.   But I couldn't go on straight, and so it's coom to this.   Sarved out, sir—just as the Bible said I should be."

He returned to his seat by the fire,

where I left him shaking his head to and fro, and muttering his complaints to that unsympathetic element.

I went into the hall, and down the broad steps into the street, where three cabmen, who had been lurking outside on the chance of a fare, made a desperate rush at me.

"Cab, ye'r honor!—cab, ye'r honor!— Hansom, ye'r honor!"

"I am going back again," I said, impatiently, as they danced round me, and swore at and jostled each other.

"The gemman's ony half-sick of it yet. Come on, Bill!"

And Bill and his confrères left me to pursue my way alone. At the corner of the next street the tall figure of Sir Richard Freemantle was plainly distinguishable. The baronet advanced to me with extended hand.

"Mr. Neider, I am obliged by your prompt response to my request."

"There is no obligation conferred, Sir Richard. Pray offer me no thanks."

" Here is a quiet coffee-house some fifty yards down the street—perhaps it will be better than talking out here in the cold.   I am somewhat of an invalid, and cold weather don't agree with me."

He shivered as he walked by my side, and remained silent until we had reached the coffee-house indicated.   Passing through its swing doors to a room at the back, more private than the first partitional compartment contiguous to the street, we took our places before a table, at which a waiter suddenly appeared for orders.   After ordering coffee, Sir Richard removed his hat, unwound a voluminous comforter from his neck, and sat waiting patiently for the waiter's reappearance and retirement before he broached the subject that had brought me face to face with him.   I removed my hat and waited with him.   I noticed that he was extremely pale, and that his hands beat nervously upon the table, until the waiter had brought the coffee and left us to ourselves.

"Now, Mr. Neider," said he, setting the coffee hastily aside, "let me give you, in detail, that news which has confounded me, and which I wish you to communicate to your friend."

"Mr. Thirsk?"

"The same. The gentleman who forbids me his house, and refuses me an audience with my only sister—who, in this hour of trial to himself, will not listen to a word of explanation."

"Have you seen him?"

"For a moment, by mere accident; but his pride would not allow him to hear a word from my lips, and I—well, I have a little pride of my own still left!"

The baronet looked more sorry than proud, I thought; I sat patiently waiting for the explanation that he seemed anxious to defer.

"Last week I received a letter from Mr. Thirsk to the effect that he had given notice to the Tramlingford Bank of his intention, as Agatha's husband, to withdraw, the day after her majority, or as soon as the needful preliminaries could be arranged, the sum of sixty thousand pounds; a sum bequeathed to her by my father, and lodged in the county bank, of which he had been a director, until such time as Agatha should reach her one and twentieth year. Do you follow me, Mr. Neider?"

"Perfectly."

"As executor to that will, I wrote to the manager of the bank of Mr. Thirsk's intention, and learned soon afterwards that your friend had already written to that effect to the manager also. All needful preliminaries were arranged, and there was nothing left but for Mr. Thirsk to receive the money when he should feel disposed to call for it, I thought."

"Thought?" I repeated.

"Mr. Neider," said the baronet, in a faltering voice, "I received a telegraphic message to-day, informing me that the bank had stopped payment!"

" Good Heavens ! "

"This was a despatch from a private friend of mine, who has awakened to the knowledge of a gigantic fraud, which the announcement of an intention to withdraw sixty thousand pounds from the deposit branch has brought suddenly to light. A fraud carried on systematically for years, and involving utter ruin to most people who have banked there. My friend followed his dispatch by express train to-night, and has told me the whole story."

" This is very bad news, Sir Richard."

"Which I wish you to communicate to Mr. Thirsk as quickly—even as gently, as possible. It must be as great a blow to *him* as can possibly occur, and one for which, in his egotism and extravagance, he is wholly unprepared. I would caution you and him from too sudden an avowal of the news to Agatha—she is a girl who has hardly known a disappointment, and would, I fear, bear but indifferently any serious shock. You will see," he added, anxiously, " that the tidings are broken to her gently ? "

" I will do my best—I have no influence with the family."

" You are his friend."

" I meet him to-night for the first time since his marriage."

" By invitation ? "

" Yes."

" I will call you his friend, then — at least he will hear more from you than me, and hear more graciously. You will warn him concerning Agatha ?"

" Certainly."

"I am deeply obliged to you, Mr. Neider ; I—I don't think I need detain you any longer. I have made you the bearer of very sad news, but I think it is news that cannot be told too soon."

" May I ask if you banked there to any extent, Sir Richard ?"

"I have lost a few thousands," he said, quietly; " fortunately I have not lost all—

thanks to my landed estate, and my investments in government securities. And fortunately for more than myself—I—I wonder if he will see a hidden motive even in that now?"

He bit his finger nails nervously a moment, then said very hastily,

"You may tell Mr. Thirsk that any embarrassments which the stoppage of the bank may necessarily involve, I shall be happy to do my best to assist him from. And that I am sorry—there, that's all."

"It is strange news to communicate on such a night as this," I remarked; "I will do my best to break it to him cautiously. But I have no great confidence in my powers, Sir Richard."

"You will excuse me making you the bearer of such news, sir," said Sir Richard, courteously.

I implied as much by a bow.

"I saw your face in the crowd after my interview with my friend," said he, "but I did not think of you again till Mr. Thirsk broke from me with an oath, and a taunt upon the mean servility that had brought me there in the zenith of his fortune. Then with some difficulty I bribed a servant to convey my pencilled note to you, and— you are here. There is the telegraphic message I received," passing it across the table.

"I can't help thinking that such news would last till the morning," said I, irresolutely, as I secured the message in my pocket.

"Ill news grows apace. Mr. Thirsk may have incurred responsibilities, and find a crowd of harpies on him in the morning, and know not where his best friends are. I shall be here all day to-morrow."

He implied by that his wish to be considered the best friend of his sister's husband; I believed that he was, and felt more sorry than ever for the enmity that Thirsk appeared to bear him. If the story ended with a better understanding between this seemingly phlegmatic, but really warm-hearted man, had Nicholas Thirsk and his wife encountered so heavy a misfortune?

I left Sir Richard at the table in the coffee-room, and went back towards the mansion. All was light and life still in the house to which I was advancing with my evil news; I could hear the music streaming out into the night —see, as I looked up, the shadows of the dancers on the blind. Feasting and revelry held domination there; the careless hearts above knew nothing of the thunderbolt launched at their host, and all his dreams of greatness. Standing on the brink of ruin, with the great abyss below, the full-hearted host recked not of the card-built castle that had gone down the gulf before him.

# CHAPTER V.

## BEFORE SUPPER.

STANDING outside the ball-room door, a new thought struck me like a pistol-shot. Matthew Genny, of Follingay Farm, near Welsdon in the Woods! He had spoken of the Tramlingford Bank; he had banked there for many years—his faith was greater in it than the Bank of England—how had the stoppage of the firm affected him?

They were questions that I could not answer, and I had a task of no small difficulty before me. For the present, I must set aside all thoughts of my old tutor in the art of farming, and bend my energies to warn Nicholas Thirsk of the storm that would descend upon him ere he was twenty-four hours older. I passed into the rooms, looking at my watch as I entered. It was twenty minutes past twelve; I had been gone an hour.

It seemed as if Nicholas Thirsk had been awaiting my return, for he was standing before me the next instant, with a lady on his arm.

" Mr. Neider," said he, with extraordinary gravity, " I have been fortunate enough to obtain Miss Winkington's consent to your desire for an introduction to her—she *is* disengaged for the next waltz. Miss Winkington—Mr. Neider; Mr. Neider—Miss Winkington!"

I stared from Nicholas Thirsk to Miss Winkington—for a few moments I did not perceive the force of Thirsk's joke, till my startled vision became aware of a formidable wen under the left ear of the lady. It was the heiress he had already recommended me!

At any other time I might have appreciated the jest, and the solemn manner in which Thirsk supported it, but I was embarrassed, and the contrast between my thoughts and his was so acutely painful

"I—I wish a word with you, Thirsk—I must speak to you a moment."

"I shall be most happy after the next dance—the music has begun again—Mr. Neider, I leave in your hands the most graceful dancer in the room."

"Naughty flatterer!" cried the lady with the wen.

"Upon my honour!" and, grave as a judge, Thirsk left me to my own resources.

There was no help for it—dance I must, and with a young lady who gave me the horrors every time I caught sight of her. It was a peculiar position—certainly the most miserable fifteen minutes I was ever likely to spend. With a load at my heart, and the knowledge of what blighting news I had to communicate, to be waltzing round a ball-room with a malformed partner, who had been told the most extraordinary account of my desire to be introduced to her !

Whether she waltzed indifferently well that night, or my feet were as heavily laden as my spirits, or the wen had something to do with it, it was certain that we laboured round the ball-room in the most lumpish and clumsy manner possible to conceive—bumping against more agile partners, falling over each other's feet, causing no small amusement to the lookers-on, and great indignation to those parties with whom we came into violent collision. If Miss Winkington would only have become disgusted with me and the attention we commanded —if the band had not played the waltz so many times over—if I could have even brought one of my heels with full force on her instep, and crippled her *pro tem.* / But she persevered, and panted and clung to me, till the last note sounded forth and the dance was over.

"It's dreadfully warm, Mr. Cyder!" observed my interesting partner, as I offered her my arm to escort her to a seat.

"Very, miss."

"The rooms are overcrowded—don't you think so?"

"I certainly do."

"I wonder the windows are not open. They have opened them in the refreshment room, and it's so delightfully cool there."

"Is it, indeed?"

But I was not to be inveigled into the refreshment room; under any other circumstances, I should have been the most gallant, the most attentive partner. But I was anxious to see Thirsk and end this burlesque, so with a "thank you" for the favour conferred, I left Miss Winkington on a seat by the wall. The contraction of a pair of very bushy eyebrows is a reminiscence with me yet, and associated with other, sterner incidents of that memorable night.

I found Thirsk after some difficulty, and seized him by the arm.

" Hollo!—here so soon! Have you enjoyed your dance ? "

" Never mind the dance—I wish to tell you something."

"Not now—I——"

"Thirsk, I must tell you what I have heard ! " I cried.

"Out with it, then !—is there murder abroad ? "

" Not quite so bad as that."

" Speak, Sir Oracle ! "

" Not here."

And I gave a scared look at the visitors promenading to and fro during the intervals of the music. He began to see that there was really something serious to relate, and led the way out of the ball-room, and along a passage to a dimly-lighted study on the same floor.

" It's not a long tale, Neider ? "

" No."

" Short and sour—go on ! "

" Are you prepared for bad news, Thirsk ? —very bad news ? "

" It must be news of awful import to dash me to-night," he said, looking anxiously towards me, as if to read the secret on my face.

" I received a message an hour and a half ago to meet Sir Richard Freemantle in the street."

" Curse it ! — why didn't I guess that that hound was at the bottom of it ? He has been here once, but I have baffled him. I have sworn never to be friends with that man—and it is my turn to wring his heart. What has he told you, Neider?—and why do you hang back so ? "

" Because you will not guess at the

shadow of a possible blow to you. Because
your wife's brother came in all good faith,
and you would not listen to him, and spare
me being the bearer of almost the worst
news I could bring."

" Well—I am prepared ! "

He turned white then, and waited for
my revelation. I believe a suspicion
of the truth for the first time came across
him.

"The Tramlingford Bank has stopped
payment !"

" So—so—so !" he repeated to himself, and
his arms fell to his side like a dead man's;
"that's news indeed ! "

" My dear Thirsk, you will not let it
dash you utterly down !" I cried; "it is not
news of death or illness to anyone you
love—it *might* have been worse."

" No."

" It might have——"

" I say No to all—don't try any damned
consolation with me; I never cared for it—

it never affected me in much less trouble! Just finish the story," he cried, with a stamp of his foot.

"Since receiving the telegraphic message——"

"Where is it?"

I placed it in his hands, and without looking at it he waited for me to continue.

"Since receiving the message," I began again, "Sir Richard's friend has arrived by the express train from Tramlingford, and entered fully into details. There has been a misappropriation of funds, a long series of artful defalcations, a reckless speculation with depositors' money, winding up, as all such things must wind up, with exposure and ruin!"

He echoed my last word, and then read the telegraphic message carefully.

"Dated half-past five o'clock at Tramlingford. That is too late for the evening papers."

"Yes."

"Well—go on."

"That's all."

"I think it's enough," he said; "and now, Neider, your congratulations."

I did not understand him, and looked my ignorance.

"Your congratulations at my stoicism—this comes of being prepared. This is not like the Follingay Farm times, when I was uncommonly quick at an explosion."

"No."

"I can hardly make it out myself," he said; "I don't realize the fact in all its grimness. I've been stunned with a heavy blow, and am not recovered yet. That's quite all, you say?"

"Excepting a few words from Sir Richard Freemantle. Shame on me if I had forgotten them!"

"Let me have his message."

"That any assistance you may need in the sudden misfortune which has befallen you, he will be happy to afford — he is most anxious to afford."

Thirsk exploded at this. There was no longer any further reason to admire his powers of self-restraint. He called down all the curses of heaven on his brother-in-law's head, and wished every evil on earth might swoop upon him for his meddling.

" Does he taunt me with his wealth again, in the very face of the ruin that he tells me of —does he think me a coward, that will spurn him in my seeming affluence, and cringe to him at the first shock of the storm? May my hand wither when I touch his own, or receive a farthing of that money which he flaunts before me as a panacea for the deadly ill he brings me news of! May the devil fly away with him!"

"This is not stoicism, Thirsk—more, it is not gratitude."

"My debt of gratitude to him was paid long ago—but my debt of hate is eternal."

"Well—what is to be done?"

"We will go on with the feast, and keep the natal day of Mrs. Thirsk."

The mocking look was in his eyes again —the mocking face was that which I had looked at, in the farming days, when he was chafing at the barriers in his way.

"But the natal day was yesterday, and the new day is an hour old, and ruin has come with it, and the supper waits. There's one striking."

"Shall I excuse you to the guests?"

"Excuse *me!*" he cried; "do you think I am a child to sit moping in a corner because the enemy has snatched my cake away. I have a part to play, Alf Neider, and you shall see me play it to perfection."

There was a wild glitter in his eyes, that might almost indicate insanity; his mood was reckless, and I knew how little he cared for form and ceremony in it. For anything wild and extravagant he was prepared—I saw it in his face. I told him so.

"It may be my only chance of getting

up a sensation for all time to come," he said.

"You will not be rash and foolish. The news may not be so bad in the morning. You have received no official intelligence, as yet, of the disaster."

"Please to let me pass," he said, haughtily; "I presume I am not to be made a prisoner in my own house."

"I have no power to make you one."

"Don't you wish you had?"

"If you think of perpetrating any foolish act that can but insult your guests, and bring no credit to yourself, I wish I had the power, Thirsk."

"The guests will flout me in the streets three days hence. Not a single craven amongst them would see me at their homes."

"Still they are your guests—asked in all fairness—to be treated fairly."

"Do you think I am going to spring a mine—à la Guido Fawkes?"

" I wouldn't be answerable for any extravagance in this darkling mood of yours."

" I see you are beginning to understand me," he said, with a short laugh.

" I wish I had the key to the better nature that I know is in you, Thirsk."

" The better nature is cast off, and the key sunk in a black river. I believe neither in heaven, nor hell, nor justice, nor God's blessing on repentant sinners, from to-night."

" Thirsk, this is cruel blasphemy !"

" Wise men who fancy they know more of retributive justice than most people— reverend old humbugs, who see the hand of Providence in everything, will say that this is a judgment upon me—a fair end to the foul scheming began years ago. There are such things as judgments, I suppose?—do you know anything about them ?"

" Judgments on what ?"

" Marrying for money. Sacrificing the

heart, and the heart's best affections—if there are such commodities—at the altar of Mammon !"

"Do you own it?" I asked, sorrowfully.

"Yes. Alfred Neider, puritan, and moralist, and farmer, I own it. I married Agatha Freemantle for money, blinding myself with the belief that I loved her a little in my own way, and that it was not all self-interest which led me in pursuit of the heiress. I might have been blind all my life, if this devil of ill-luck—there is such a devil as that always on the watch for us—had not torn the bandage from my eyes. I married her for money !"

"I will not believe anything you say to-night."

"I married her for money !" he repeated again; "she was worth sixty thousand pounds, and that would have made a man of me. I have been kind to her for her money—I give this fête to-day, not that she is one-and-twenty, but that I hoped to shake away the fetters at my heels, and step forth into society a rich man. And I am balked, and society will laugh at me !"

" If you *would* only let me say that you are unwell, and——"

" Let me be," he interrupted, " I have every confidence in myself. What I do shall be done like a gentleman, not like a butcher. Who's there?"

A hand without tapped upon the panels of the door.

" If you please, mistress wishes to know if you will be long, sir. It is past one."

" I know it, scaramouch," was the un-complimentary rejoinder ; " now, Mr. Nei-der, *apres vous.*"

I still looked irresolutely at him.

" You are a strangely suspicious mortal —forward !"

" What do you intend?"

" Nothing, nothing — haven't I heard you say that you are an admirer of William Shakspere's works?"

" I daresay you have."

" That's a grand satire on money worship-
pers and against sycophants—that Timon of
Athens, Neider."

" What of it ?"

" Nothing much — you remember the
wind-up in the third act ? "

" What of it ?" I repeated.

" That's a grand dash at the dish-covers,
and a denunciation to the purpose on the
heads of the many who would have fattened
at the host's expense, and fallen down at his
feet to worship him."

" Did he act like a gentleman ?"

" Ah ! for the times that he lived in. I
am Thirsk of Bedford Square—not Timon
of Athens !"

He passed his arm through mine, and led
me along the passage, and back into the
ball-room. I was distrustful of him still—
doubtful, after all, if the shock of his loss had
not been a little too much for him.

At the door of the ball-room Mrs. Thirsk
met him with a wondering face.

" Nicholas, dear — where have you been ? "

" Playing at nine-pins with Mr. Neider."

" What ? "

And the young wife stared at him, as she well might.

" And Neider's beaten me. Such a floorer in one throw—you should have seen it—it would have vastly amused you ! "

" Shall I give the signal to open the doors of the supper-room ? "

" By all means—our guests must be hungry."

They were standing in groups about the room, laughing and talking. Those who had come for supper especially—there are such social wolves—were becoming a little impatient.

" Neider, may I place Mrs. Thirsk under your charge ? "

" With great pleasure—but——"

" But my best friends have a right to

take the best position—I have only a few more honours to bestow in this life."

When Mrs. Thirsk's hand rested on my arm, he said—

" By the way, I had forgotten Miss Winkington—if you have any *penchant* in that direction, I will waive my own desires."

" No," I said.

It was grim jesting, and Thirsk's pleasantry at that time made my blood run cold.

" Don't be frightened," I heard him whisper behind me, as we passed into the supper-room.

END OF THE SECOND VOLUME.